The Irish Theatre Series 4
Edited by Robert Hogan, James Kilroy *and* Liam Miller

The Playboy Riots

The 'Playboy' Riots

by James Kilroy

The Dolmen Press

Set in Times Roman type, and printed and published in the Republic of Ireland at the Dolmen Press, 8 Herbert Place, Dublin 2.

1971

Distributed outside Ireland, except in the U.S.A. and in Canada by Oxford University Press

SBN 85105 199 5

Introduction

Riots in the theatre; members of the audience ejected or arrested for crying out against an immoral play; editorials protesting an alleged libel on Ireland: these are proof of the excitement of the Irish theatre in January 1907, when John M. Synge's The Playboy of the Western World *was first performed. Several generations later we may well be surprised that such an uproar could have been set off by a play now accepted as a masterpiece of comedy. But in the early years of this century, theatre riots, although not common, were certainly not rare. Just a year before a more violent uproar had occurred during an act by, of all things, a cowboy hypnotist:*

Belfast, Friday, 2 February, 1906

To-night at the Palace of Varieties sensational scenes were witnessed when Ahrensmayer, known as 'the Cowboy Hypnotist', was in the process of hypnotising a young lady. He placed upon the lady's chest a stone, which he invited any member of the audience to come forward and smash, and his invitation was immediately accepted by a gentleman present, who was, however, objected to by those in the gallery and pit, from which a storm of yells and cries of dissatisfaction proceeded. The other parts of the house joined in the uproar. An ugly rush was made towards the stage, and the crowd broke into the orchestra and smashed the instruments of the musicians. The fire-proof screen was lowered, and thereupon the crowd proceeded to demolish the decorations and ornaments and tear in pieces the electrical fittings. The cinematograph apparatus was broken up, and chairs were flung into the stalls. The scene was one of wild disorder and excitement for about half an hour, and the row was only quelled when fifty police were marched in. The police succeeded in clearing the building, but by that time a considerable amount of property had been wrecked and demolished.[1]

A campaign against that staple of popular comedies, the stage Irishman, had taken shape, so that any supposed affront to the noble Irish was likely to evoke hostility. The nationalist movement was growing and its adherents were naturally hypersensitive to any questioning of their nation's virtues. And slights against holy Ireland on the stage had already brought violent responses. As early as 1899, when Yeats's

5

The Countess Cathleen *was first performed in Dublin, there were vocal protests in the theatre and outraged petitions in the newspapers for days following. Even outside of Dublin, in Liverpool and St. Louis, there had been disturbances in theatres triggered by alleged attacks on Ireland or offensive representations of the Irish character. The very week that these riots broke out in Dublin, a similar scene—hisses, cat-calls and jeers of an organized pro-Irish audience—forced the Russell Brothers off the stage of Hammerstein's Victoria Theatre in New York for their alleged ridicule of the Irish.*

But for all the precedents, this riot had far greater effects. It resulted in a changed audience, a loss of support from the Nationalist group, and the temporary withdrawal of the Abbey's most popular dramatist, William Boyle. Important as its historical effects are, the Playboy riots merit renewed study as they reveal a number of continuing issues. Much of the dissension voiced in the editorials, letters and public statements stems from disagreement over just what a national theatre should be. To the nationalist, the issues were simple: a national theatre should serve as an instrument of propaganda; clearly this production was not flattering to Ireland; it must, then, be anti-Irish. Even to those less committed to political causes, it seemed irrational for the directors of what called itself a national theatre to persist in showing a play which the leading newspapers and most of the audience found repulsive. Those arguments that the playwright should serve his audience and not defy its opinions are all too familiar today. Finally, there occurs in these discussions the still unresolved question of the author's license both in using realistic but shocking language and in frankly treating distasteful subjects. In other words, the issues raised are central questions of literary criticism and aesthetics.

But in our consideration of these historical and artistic problems, we cannot ignore the sheer pleasure of reading these earnest and often angry statements: the shocking play was the occasion of lively disagreement and not a little bit of good humour.

*   *   *

Contemporary newspaper accounts and first-hand reports are the most accurate sources for determining the facts of the Playboy riots and understanding its issues. They convey the excitement of the events and the tone of the controversy in a manner that defies mere paraphrasing.

6

The 'Playboy' Riots

The Playboy of the Western World *opened on Saturday, 26 January, 1907, for a run scheduled to continue through the following Saturday. The opening night audience was large; advance publicity and Synge's reputation drew the leaders of Dublin political and artistic circles. But protests against the supposed immorality of such plays as* In the Shadow of the Glen *were increasing, and the involvement of Yeats and his associates in the political movement was being questioned. There were hints that a battle might be due.*

The first shots were fired on Monday, 28 January, 1907, by The Freeman's Journal. *Its vehement and damning review sets forth most of the charges to be repeated against the play: its slander against Ireland, its obscenity, its inauthenticity, and its inappropriateness to the Dublin stage:*

The Abbey Theatre is now seriously and widely recognised as a home of drama. The culture and thoughtfulness of its large and growing clientele would alone give importance to doings upon its boards. It is, therefore, necessary to take notice of things which, if done elsewhere, might possibly be dismissed on the principle that least said is soonest mended. Even in this case, one is tempted to be curt regarding the performance of Saturday night last, for it is very difficult to write with patience of J. M. Synge's piece, 'The Playboy of the Western World'. A strong protest must, however, be entered against this unmitigated, protracted libel upon Irish peasant men and, worse still, upon Irish peasant girlhood. The blood boils with indignation as one recalls the incidents, expressions, ideas of this squalid, offensive production, incongruously styled a comedy in three acts. Lest these censures might appear unfair and uncalled for, a brief indication must be given of what it is all about. The action takes place in a publichouse, on a wild part of the coast of Mayo. The publican, with some companions, is bound for a wake. His young unmarried daughter is to be left alone all night. A footsore, travel-stained fellow is discovered lurking near the house. One Shawn Keogh is making sheep's eyes at Margaret, the publican's daughter. He, however, is but a whining, cowardly lout. The tramp enters and reveals that he is apprehensive of the police. He believes he has murdered his father in a distant county, and has been evading pur-

7

suit. He tells how they had quarrelled when digging potatoes, and how he struck him on the head with a weapon and killed him. Instantly Christy Mahon, that is his name, becomes a hero not only with the men, but with the girl Margaret. He must be a brave, daring, splendid fellow to have done such a terrific deed. On the spot he is engaged as pot-boy, and is left to keep Margaret company in the publichouse while the others set off for their midnight spree. Margaret's shocking unnatural love for the supposed murderer develops. The repulsive theme is made the basis of what the author esteems his comedy. Mahon's fame soon spreads. The Widow Quin is smitten. She tries to snatch the treasure from Margaret. A gruesome rivalry is set up for the assassin. Other peasant girls also come to admire and make much of him. He himself fixes on Margaret. He is too comfortable in the publichouse to fall into the widow's wiles. Margaret sternly resents any others' attempts on the affections of her strong fearless young man. Her fearful love is based on a brutish admiration of his lethal prowess. She would not be afraid to go with such one poaching salmon by night in the country streams. Mahon's popularity is so great that the peasants must have him in their sports, which take place on the shore the day following his arrival. Meanwhile his father turns up. His head is bandaged. He is swearing vengeance on his son. The Widow Quin tries to get him off the scene. The sports take place. Mahon conquers all before him. The people, male and female, are delighted. Margaret's passion is at the full. Old Mahon again appears, confronts all and denounces Christy. Margaret's idol is shattered. He is not a murderer after all. His bragging was but a lie. The people round upon him. Margaret's resentment is furious. She assails him with fiendish vehemence. He pursues his father, apparently again beats him, and is followed by the peasants, who proceed to tie him with a rope. The audience had stood this revolting story thus far. Now angry groans, growls, hisses, and noise broke out while the pinioning of Mahon went on. It was not possible—thank goodness—to follow the dialogue for a time. Mahon springs forward and bites the leg of one of his captors—his rival Shawn. The girls and others rush in with the father, now in his shirt sleeves and brandishing a weapon. A brutal riotous scene takes place. The groans, hisses, and counter cheers of the audience drowned the words, but as well as could be gathered Christy decides to depart quietly with his father, and let Mayo resume its normal state of sickening demoralisation. The mere idea can be given of the barbarous jargon, the elaborate and incessant cursings of these repulsive creatures. Everything is a b————y this or a ————y that, and into this picturesque dialogue names that should only be used with respect and reverence are frequently introduced. Enough! the hideous caricature would be slanderous of a Kaffir kraal. The piece is announced to run for a week; it is to be hoped it will be instantly withdrawn. If a company of English artistes attempted such an outrage the public indignation would be rightly bitter. Indeed no denunciation could be sufficiently strong. The whole affair is absolutely incomprehensible however it is examined. That such a piece should have been conceived and written is strange enough; that it could be accepted, rehearsed, and enacted at a house supposed to be dedicated to high dramatic art and truth would be past all belief but that it has actually been done. The worst specimen of stage Irishman of the past is a refined, acceptable fellow compared with that imagined by Mr. Synge. and as for his women, it is not possible, even if it were desirable, to class them. Redeeming features may be found in the dregs of humanity. Mr. Synge's dramatis personae stand apart in complete and forbidding isolation. It is not necessary to inquire whether, even if such things were true, they should be brought upon the stage. It is quite plain that there is need for a censor at the Abbey Theatre.[1]

Following this review come the first of many pseudonymous letters of outrage. A few vague sentences purport to be pure dramatic criticism, but the authoress only repeats the usual charges, adding the first protest against the utterance of that shocking word 'shifts'. It seems to have been Pegeen's utterance of the word in Act II, that upset the writer even more than Christy's mention of it in the last act:

DEAR SIR—As an Irishwoman, I desire to enter a most emphatic protest against Mr. J. M. Synge's new comedy, 'The Playboy of the Western World'.

I am well acquainted with the conditions of life in the West, and not only does this play not truly represent these conditions, but it portrays the people of that part of Ireland as a coarse, besotted race, without one gleam of genuine humour or one sparkle of virtue. . . .

We have now an Irish dramatist putting on the boards of a Dublin theatre a play representing Irish people actively sympathising with a

9

parricide, while Irish girls fling themselves into his arms, and an Irish peasant woman, who has made herself a widow, proving herself to be a liar, an intriguer, and a coarse-spoken virago, whose honesty is purchasable at the price of a red cow. Could any Irish person accept this as a true picture of Irish life? Fancy such a play being produced in England!

There is nothing to show that this picture is not to be taken seriously. I think I know the West of Ireland as well as Mr. Synge does, and I can state that in no part of the South or West would a parricide be welcomed. Not only would such a man be shunned, but his brothers, sisters, and blood relations would be more or less boycotted for generations. Is it necessary for me to say that in no part of Ireland are the women so wanting in modesty as to make advances to a total stranger, much less to a criminal?

Nothing redeems the general sordidness of the piece. Every character uses coarse expressions, and Miss Allgood (one of the most charming actresses I have ever seen) is forced, before the most fashionable audience in Dublin, to use a word indicating an essential item of female attire, which the lady would probably never utter in ordinary circumstances, even to herself.

Considered merely as a play the piece is feeble. There is nothing to sustain the interest, and the fate of any of the characters is a matter of indifference to the spectator.

The play is stilted, impossible, uninteresting, and un-Irish. It is a pity that the Messrs. Fay, Miss Allgood, Miss O'Neill, Mr. Power, and the other capable members of this excellent company should for once, through no fault of their own, find themselves unable to please their audience. I understand that the play was produced for the first time on Saturday night—let us hope it will be for the last.

Lest it should be thought that this letter disingenuous, I may mention that I am in entire sympathy with the efforts to create a National drama, and that I have been a supporter of the Abbey Theatre since it has been devoted to the representation of Irish folk life.

Yours truly,
A WESTERN GIRL 2

The other reviews in daily newspapers are far less heated. Each praises the acting of W. G. Fay and the supporting players, and each has some qualified praise for other aspects of the production. The

Daily Express, *for instance, finds the dialogue 'in many parts sparkling and witty. It would, perhaps, be the better for some slight revision here and there, particularly in the third act in which there is a sentence, spoken by the hero, which gave rise to an emphatic expression of dissent from the gallery, and which nobody could say was not justified'. But the central situation—the adulation of the playboy by the Mayo women—this seems unlikely:*

Now this Christy, a curious-looking little scamp, is an object upon whom the Widow Quin and two or three other girls have set their affections. What they could possibly have seen in him would have puzzled the indifferent; and why, above all, they should excite each other's jealousy over a self-confessed parricide, the author alone can explain. It can scarcely be true that Irish girls contend for murderers as husbands.[3]

Possibly because of the disturbances in the theatre on even the opening night, the important reversal at the end of the play, in which Christy Mahon denounces the Mayo peasants and goes off, 'a likely gaffer in the end of all', victorious over his audience and his father, was missed by the reviewers. Thus the central theme of the play, the growth of the playboy through his encounter with Pegeen and the Mayo crowd, is not recognized in the early reviews.

The first short review in the Irish Times *is also guarded in its praise of the play's realism, and restrained in its criticism of the surprising dialogue:*

The majority of theatre-goers are not accustomed to 'remorseless truth' in characterisation, and after witnessing 'The Playboy' they will be rather strenghtened than otherwise in their preference for the conventional form of stage representation. Mr. Synge set himself the task of introducing his audience to a realistic picture of peasant life in the far west of Ireland, and he succeeded in accomplishing his purpose with a remarkable degree of success. . . . There is much to commend in Mr. Synge's work, but it is open to serious question whether he has been well advised in regard to some of the dialogue. While there is not a word or a turn of expression in the play that is not in common use amongst peasants, it is quite another matter to reproduce some of the expressions on a public stage in a large city. People here will not publicly approve of the indiscriminate use of the

Holy Name on every possible occasion, nor will they quietly submit to the reproduction of expressions which, to say the least, are offensive to good taste, however true they may be to actual life.[4]

The Irish Independent *echoes these objections to the shocking dialogue of the play, but also recognizes some substance in its theme:*

There need be no hesitation in saying that 'The Playboy of the Western World' is at least the work of a writer with ideas, although he still lacks the skill to put them into acceptable shape. Every playwright is at the outset confronted with two grave difficulties, the choice of a subject and the manner in which that subject shall be treated. In respect of the first Mr. Synge has been fairly happily inspired; it is in connection with the second that he comes to grief. . . . Through the three acts the story is told with such a light touch through crisp and sparkling, sometimes rather coarse, dialogue as tends to amuse the audience, and by inciting their laughter at its pungent witticism prevents them from thinking of the social incongruities masked behind the play of words. But the whole thing is impossible. Peasants who look and act like omadhauns don't suddenly develop a passion for killing their fathers as easily as Mr. Synge would have us believe.

Most emphatically, the reviewer objects to the character of Christy as a familiar and insulting stock character:

His playboy, it is safe to say, has not his equal in Ireland. He is certainly not a type to be presented even in farce in an Irish theatre, and under the auspices of a movement that has for its very object the destruction of such stage-Irishman types as Christie [sic] Mahon. . . . How would it be, say, if such a type of stage Irishman appeared in a play brought across-Channel and presented in Dublin? Wouldn't there be an uproar, and wouldn't the uproar be all the greater if the author seriously affirmed that his delineations of characters and incidents were true to Irish life?[5]

This particular objection to the stage Irishman would evoke fury from the young Nationalists of this time, for one of their campaigns had been directed against the offensive Paddys so common in popular English plays.

12

But 'H. S. D.', *the reviewer in the* Evening Mail, *although finding serious faults with its structure and its message, cites the very absence of stage Irish exaggerations as a redeeming quality to the play:*

'The Playboy of the Western World' is a remarkable achievement, a comedy brilliantly written, and brilliantly acted. The story is simple, and, it must be said at once,

ENTIRELY UNCONVINCING.

That is why I say it is brilliantly written rather than brilliantly constructed. We leave the theatre entirely unconvinced that such a thing could have happened. Mr. Synge's triumph is that he has given us a grotesque story, and so presented it that we listen to its unfolding, drinking in every word of the dialogue with eager and excited interest, and captivated by the rare charm and reality of the sayings and manners of his wonderful living Irish peasants, and cheerfully indifferent to the unreality of their actions and motives. . . . It is . . . absurd and un-Irish, and smacks of the decadent ideas of the literary flaneurs of Paris rather than of simple Connaught; or, perhaps, it is an allegory, and the parricide represents some kind of nation-killer, whom Irishmen and Irish women hasten to lionise. If it is an allegory it is too obscure for me. I cannot stalk this alligator on the banks of the Liffey. But the telling of this story is supremely clever. Mr. Synge's Irish peasants—putting aside their absurd motives—are wonderful. It is a far cry from the stage Irishman, who outraged the Irish visitors to the Pike at St. Louis, to Myles-na-Coppaleen. It is an equally far cry from the comic Irishman of Dion Boucicault to the Christie [sic] Mahon of Mr. Synge. Christie is the living, breathing Irish peasant, unsoiled by contact with the world beyond his own barony, Mr. Synge's literary craftsmanship is marvellous. His peasants' talk is racy of the soil. . . . I do not see any reason for working myself into a state of pallid indignation at Mr. Synge's preposterous theory that Irish peasant girls fall in love at first sight with the worst type of murderers. It is merely foolish; and a compassionate shrug of the shoulders is adequate comment. If a man is stupid enough to suggest that the Irish people are cannibals or gorillas, my hand will not fumble for the sword hilt. . . . But there is one thing worth protesting against—occasional indelicacy in the dialogue. . . . Mr. Synge may have been pulling our leg with his

13

theme, and we are not going to gratify him with indignation. But we do resent it, when, having given proof of brilliant powers of dialogue, he deliberately assails our ears with coarse or blasphemous language. Mr. Synge is himself, apparently, 'The Playboy of the Western World': he will be more welcome if he moderates his transports.[6]

Except for the Freeman's Journal *review, the first day's reviews are not so denunciatory as to provoke or even encourage the riots which followed. But Monday night's performance was the scene of unparallelled disorder:*

THE ABBEY THEATRE.

UPROARIOUS SCENES.

PROTESTS AGAINST MR. SYNGE'S PLAY.

SPEECH OF MR. W. G. FAY.

THE POLICE CALLED IN.

POLICE ACTED IN DUMB SHOW.

Last night the Abbey Theatre was the scene of a demonstration of a character which has not been witnessed in Dublin for a considerable period. In a very thin house, Saturday night's programme, 'Riders to the Sea' and 'The Playboy of the Western World', was repeated. Owing to circumstances which it would be superfluous to dilate on, the occasion was regarded in certain circles with intense interest. Although the audience collectively was of small dimensions, the pit was very congested. 'Riders to the Sea' was most favourably received. For a few minutes after 'The Playboy of the Western World' had been begun the rather smart dialogue was applauded. But an extraordinary change soon occurred. Hisses testified to the disapprobation of the house at the manner in which the self-accused parricide, Christopher Mahon (Mr. W. G. Fay), was taken to the arms of the Western peasants. This hostile manifestation reached an acute stage when it was decided that Mahon was to remain during the night in Flaherty's publichouse, the only other inmate of which would be the publican's daughter, Margaret (Maire O'Neill).

14

Now, the uproar assumed gigantic dimensions, stamping, boohing, vociferations in Gaelic, and the striking of seats with sticks were universal in the gallery and pit. Amidst this Babel of sounds the refrain of 'God Save Ireland' was predominant.

Loud shouts were also raised of 'We won't have this'. 'It is not good enough for Dublin', and 'What would not be tolerated in America will not be allowed here'.

MR. FAY'S SPEECH.

Mr. W. G. Fay now came forward to the footlights. He was the recipient of anything but a cordial reception. When a sort of comparative calm had been obtained,

Mr. Fay said—Now, as you are all tired, I suppose I may speak (boos, and yells of 'We won't have it.')

Mr. Fay—There are people here who have paid to see the piece. Anyone who does not like the play can have his money returned.

Cries of 'Irishmen do not harbour murderers'.

A Voice—We respect Irish virtue.

Mr. Fay—Who are the men who speak about Irish virtue? Let the play go on to the end of the act. I say again you can get your money back. We don't want to keep it. There are people who want to see the play. If they are not permitted to do so I will pull the curtain down, and have the disturbers removed. The piece will be played.

A Voice—If you don't pull the curtain down we will pull it down for you (deafening cheers).

Cries were then raised of 'Where is the author? Bring him out, and we will deal with him.'

Mr. Fay—What do you want the author for? You can have your money back.

Hundreds of Voices—We don't want the money. It is a libel on the National Theatre. We never expected this of the Abbey.

Amidst the tumultuous applause which followed, cries of 'Sinn Fein for ever' were strenuously uttered.

A Voice—Such a thing as is represented could not occur in Ireland.

A gentleman whose proclivities were not exactly on the popular side rose and shouted—'What about Mullinahone and the witch-burning?'

This query was responded to by very emphatic execrations.

15

Mr. Fay—You have not won. I will send for the police, and every man who kicks up a row will be removed.

Cries of—'Send for them; we will meet them.'

The curtain was now drawn, about half of the first act having been gone through, the uproar having lasted for more than a quarter of an hour.

The partial cessation of the performance was hailed with triumphant cheers from the demonstrants.

But now a new phase was entered on, which excited more or less expectancy. The police unquestionably had been sent for.

To while away the time, the band resumed their places in the orchestra and recommenced playing. They might, however, have spared themselves the trouble. The sounds they educed from their instruments were drowned by the singing of verses in Irish, and also the enthusiastic rendering of 'Hurrah for the Men of the West.'

After the lapse of a quarter of an hour close on a dozen policemen entered the theatre and took up a position commanding the left side of the pit, whilst another body of constables were stationed outside the building. Their advent was hailed with a torrent of boohs.

The performance was now resumed.

Mr. Fay again addressed the house, stating the action of the dissentients was very bad, and repeating that if they did not like the play their money would be refunded.

Voices—We are not afraid. We protest against the play going on. We won't have it.

Amidst boohing and other conceivable and almost inconceivable noises, the action of the drama was proceeded with. It was mere dumb show so far as the artistes were concerned. Not a syllable they spoke could be heard. At last the curtain descended on the conclusion of the first section of the production, amidst howls, cheers, and the singing of National songs.

Now the unexpected occurred. As the result of some apparently mystic sign or command, the constables turned right about and marched in stately style out of the building.

Needless is it to state that the victorious occupants of the pit and gallery signalised their success by triumphant yells, shouts, tramping of feet, and the belabouring of seats and walls with sturdy sticks, mingled with the singing of 'The West's Awake,' 'A Nation Once Again,' and such like well-known patriotic compositions, in which nearly all the audience joined.

16

At ten o'clock, the curtain was raised on the second act. Once more the performance was merely pantomimic owing to the hurricane of hissing with which it was greeted.

A similar fate awaited the presentation of the third act.

For fully five minutes after the play had concluded the building was the scene of great animation and excitement. Those who had objected to the entertainment gave effect to their elation in energetic outbursts in both Irish and English on the success they had achieved, and energetically declared that they would adopt a similar attitude on every occasion the play would be produced.

Mr. Fay, in the middle of the closing incidents, came forward and said—'Those people who are here to-night will say, "We heard this play—"' (Cries of 'We have heard enough') during which Mr. Fay retired.[7]

So chaotic was the scene that reports of what happened vary. The Irish Independent *reports that Synge and Lady Gregory dismissed the police, and describes the second act disturbance thus:*

The act went on, but not a soul in the place heard a word, so great was the din created by the folk in the gallery.

The latter sang songs, hissed, called the policemen names, denounced the players, invited the author to a free fight, and before the act was over the curtain went down amidst terrific hissing and booing. There were again cries for the author, but he did not come forward; and Mr. Fay, coming to the footlights, said something which was not audible, and the curtain went down again amidst cheers.

THE AUTHOR APPEARS.

At this juncture Lady Gregory and the author of the play entered the auditorium, and there were again cries for the author's speech. Mr. Synge, who took his seat near the orchestra, when asked by a reporter if he would say anything, replied that he was suffering from influenza, and could not speak; and owing to the rigorous cries of the audience he was obliged to leave the auditorium.

The final act was then proceeded with, but no one in the house heard a word of it owing to the din created by the audience, many of whom cried—'Sinn Fein'; 'Sinn Fein Amhain'—and 'Kill the Author'. Still the author was adamant, and despite many personal calls to him, he

17

refused to make a speech, and the final curtain fell amid a scene of great disorder in the house.

Speaking to a representative of the 'Independent' after the performance, Mr. Synge announced his intention of producing the comedy each night during the week. 'There is nothing in it,' he added, 'that we have reason to be ashamed of. We simply claim the liberty of Art to choose what subjects we think fit to put on.' Lady Gregory, who was standing by, assented.[8]

The demonstration was so unexpected and so prolonged that it seemed deliberately organized. The writer for the Dublin Evening Mail *certainly assumes that it was:*

The extraordinary disturbance in the Abbey Theatre last night must be regarded by well-wishers of the Irish drama as a distinctly 'regrettable incident.' Mr. J. M. Synge's new comedy, 'The Playboy of the Western World', may afford material for controversy, but that is no reason why it should not be played, and the organised attempt to prevent the performance is nothing to the credit of the disturbers. In Ireland we profess to be as fond of fair play as other people, and without going into the merits or demerits of the piece, we think all decent people will agree that Mr. Synge's former work has at least earned for him the claim to a fair show. We are far from attempting to limit the right of an audience to express its disapproval of any performance, but we are opposed to organised demonstrations of the kind that took place last night, and the public will agree with us that the conduct of those who listened quietly to the piece at its first production on Saturday evening, and returned last night for no other purpose than that of creating a disturbance, was in the highest degree objectionable. Having seen the play and formed an unfavourable opinion of it, all they had a legitimate right to do was to stay away, and tell their friends what they thought of the piece; and why. If 'The Playboy of the Western World' is not a good play, or if it contains anything objectionable, it will meet the same fate as other productions which have not captured the favour of the public. We have sufficient confidence in the judgement of Dublin audiences to predict that they will not continue to give support to a play which is not worth seeing. On the other hand, we are certain they will not be deterred from going because a mean attempt has been made to terrorise the players, and prevent the Dublin theatre-going public forming its own opinion.[9]

But the Freeman's Journal, *which had railed against the first performance, was equally outraged that the managers of the theatre chose to continue its run as scheduled:*

With an audacity worthy of a better cause, 'The Playboy of the Western World, was produced again last night in the theatre in Abbey Street that styles itself Irish and National. In an interview with our representative, Lady Gregory and the author, Mr. Synge, expressed their determination to insist on presenting it every night for the rest of the week. It is impossible to understand the reason that prompts this continued outrage not merely on National feeling, but on truth and decency. It is not too much to say that no traducer of the Irish people ever presented a more sordid, squalid, and repulsive picture of Irish life and character. It is calumny gone raving mad. Why it was written, why it was accepted and rehearsed and produced, and why the management insist on reproducing it in the teeth of all protest, are problems for which it is impossible to hint a solution. The Abbey Theatre has often declared its mission is to elevate the Irish drama, to banish the stage Irishman from the theatre. But the stage Irishman is a gentleman in comparison with the vile wretch whom Mr. Synge presented to an astonished Irish audience as the most popular type of Western peasant. The chief faults of the ordinary stage Irishman are excessive flamboyance and curious eccentricities of costume and brogue. But the Abbey street stage Irishman, for whom the other is ordered to make way, is a foul-mouthed scoundrel and parricide. . . .

The 'Evening Mail', indeed, considers this gross calumny on Irish life, character, and feeling a subject rather for contempt than indignation. . . .

We do not think that this attitude of easy indifference can be safely adopted. Grossness of language is, of course, an offence to be condemned. But the calumny on the Irish people, of which the whole play is an embodiment, deserves still more scathing condemnation. Let us remember this calumny runs on old and familiar lines. It has ever been the custom of traducers of the Irish people to charge them with sympathy with all forms of crime. Over and over again this same lie has been made the justification for Coercion. To those who think that the calumny in Mr. Synge's play be safely condoned as too grotesque to be offensive may be commended the views of the 'Irish Times', which commends the squalid and repulsive travesty as 'remorseless truth', even to the profane and foul-mouthed dialogue. . . . For right appreciation of the position it is essential to remember the mission for which the promoters of the Abbey Street theatre invited the sympathy of the Irish people. They were expected to fulfil the true purpose of playing— 'to hold as 'twere the mirror up to Nature', to banish the meretricious stage, and give, for the first time, true pictures of Irish life and a fulfilment of that pledge. If these be the real Irish men and women, the worst that has been said of them by their bitterest traducers has been too charitable. Do those who insist on its production claim that it is true to Irish life? The question demands an answer. Last night the indignant protest of the audience was met by an offer to return their money. On the continuance of the protest the management called in the police. It was a curious spectacle: an Irish National Theatre persisting under police protection in outraging an Irish audience. The production of the play might be pardoned if it were promptly withdrawn. But persistence in reproducing it commits all concerned with the Theatre to approval of this very gross and wanton insult to the Irish people.[10]

Joseph Holloway, in his journal, reports that it was not only Synge and Lady Gregory who were firm in their determination to continue performances despite the violent reaction:

Tuesday 29 January 1907: Went down to the Abbey on business in the morning and found the players all agog about the events of last night, and defending the play and pitching in to the audience for their behaviour. . . . All connected with the theatre seem bent on slaying its prospect of future success by persisting in playing the piece for the balance of the week, despite the wishes of the theatre's patrons.[11]

As is evident, even Holloway was disturbed at the apparent morbidity and falsity of the play.
F. S. S. [Francis Sheehy-Skeffington] in a letter to the Irish Times *finds serious fault with the play, but implies that it should be presented for the remainder of the week as scheduled:*

SIR,—My excuse for venturing to put forward publicly my unfavourable impression of 'The Playboy of the Western World' is that I have been for over three years an enthusiastic admirer of Mr. Synge's work. I have witnessed the first performance of each of his three previous plays—'The Shadow of the Glen', 'Riders to the Sea', and

'The Well of the Saints'—and I have, in various little academes, ardently and consistently championed these dramas against those who charge them with unreality, morbidity, libelling the Irish character, and so forth. When Mr. Yeats, speaking at University College a couple of years ago, declared that the battle for dramatic freedom in Ireland was destined to rage around Mr. Synge—when he prophesied for Mr. Synge a European reputation in twenty years' time—I shared that opinion and concurred in the prophesy. And I do still—that is why I take the liberty of uttering a friendly warning to Mr. Synge, in the hope that the unfavourable criticism of his admirers may induce him to refrain from wasting his capacities on work unworthy of him, and thus retarding the fulfilment of Mr. Yeats' prophesy.

'The Playboy of the Western World' is described as a comedy, but its 'humour' is of such a low and vulgar type as to disgust, not to amuse, any mind of ordinary refinement and good taste. This does not apply, I hasten to say, to the first act, which contains much genuinely humorous writing, and which was received with general applause by Saturday night's audience. But the promise of this act is woefully belied by its successors. The second and third acts were listened to with growing impatience and irritation. As another spectator put it to me, they are written in 'the languages of the gutter, with just a touch of quaintness'. The quaintness could not long keep at bay the disgust of the spectators at the growing coarseness of the dialogue. I am not squeamish, and have no puritanical objection to strong language on the stage, provided it can be made to subserve an artistic purpose. But here it appeared to be gratuitously dragged in, as if the author had set himself to find out exactly how much his audience would stand. If that were his object, he achieved it. One particularly objectionable phrase, towards the close of the third act, snapped their strained patience, and the remainder of the play was only audible in fragments above the noise of vigorous groaning and counter-cheering. Personally, I took part in neither, my predominant feeling being one of regret at Mr. Synge's bad taste; but I must say that, in my opinion, the hostile demonstration, manifestly spontaneous and sincere, was thoroughly justified and distinctly healthy.

There are other faults in 'The Playboy'. It is badly constructed, and is too thin for three acts; it shows in a marked degree that obsession by the sexual idea which is the obverse of one of Mr. Synge's qualities; it overdoes the grotesque in character and incident. But these, though

21

legitimate subjects of criticism, would not of themselves have provoked open attack, as this deliberate vulgarity did. Of course, we must preserve due measure in our condemnation. There is no pantomime or musical comedy which is not, in its veneered grossness, many times more offensive to any cultivated taste than 'The Playboy'. But the Abbey Theatre audience is a thinking one, and takes its drama seriously; and it is well for the future of Irish dramatic art that it should be so. I hope, however, that no one interested in Irish drama will condemn 'The Playboy' at second-hand. It will be produced all this week, and there is ample opportunity for theatre-going Dublin to form an opinion independent of any published criticisms. The excellent work Mr. Synge has already done entitles him to so much consideration from the public. But should the final verdict prove definitely hostile, should the audiences of the week endorse the view so forcibly expressed on Saturday, then, I submit, 'The Playboy' ought to be permanently withdrawn from the boards, and Mr. Synge should prepare to do some work really worthy of his talents.

This is not a general critique of the performance, so I have nothing to add about the admirable acting which vainly endeavoured to save the play from censure. I sincerely hope Mr. Synge will not again subject Mr. Fay and his company to such an ordeal. Yours, etc. . . .

F. S. S.[12]

It was over this action, continuing the play's run despite the violent reactions of an audience, that the most fierce disputes developed. After all, it was argued, the theatre exists to supply whatever the audience favours, and a national theatre is even more dependent on the wishes of its public.

In the tumult which followed Monday night's performance, an earnest reporter for the Dublin Evening Mail *secured a rather frantic interview with Synge:*

Mr. Synge, who had promised me half an hour after the play was over, was scarcely in a mood for being interviewed. He looked excited and restless, the perspiration standing out in great beads over his forehead and cheeks, and, besides, he seemed just then in extraordinary demand by sundry persons, who had all sorts of things to say to him. I practically had to collar him and drag him away with me to some quiet spot. But the quietest I could find was the narrow passage leading up to the stage from the entrance hall, and that was anything but quiet. We were continually jostled and interrupted, and the draughts, too, were blowing from all directions, but I was not going to grumble. I was conscious of the one thing only—that I had cornered my man, and must have it out with him. Neither was there any time to waste; so I began straight away.

'Tell me, Mr. Synge, was your purpose in writing this play to represent Irish life as it is lived—in short, did you think yourself holding up the mirror to nature?'

'No, no', Mr. Synge answered, rather emphatically.

That was going in direct opposition to the first rule laid down by the foremost playwright. But another Irish playwright before Mr. Synge has already put Shakespeare to shame, if we are to put our faith in what George Moore said of some of the plays of Edward Martyn; only it may be that not many of us have got this faith.

'What, then, was your object in this play?' I asked after a while.

'Nothing', Mr. Synge answered, with sustained emphasis, due probably to his excited condition, 'simply the idea appealed to me—it pleased myself, and I worked it up'.

'But do you see now how it displeases others? And did you ever think, when writing it, how it would be received by the public?'

"I never thought of it—HI!' to one of the attendants, who was brushing past us, 'See the police are there ready to quell the row'— then turning to myself,

'IT DOES NOT MATTER A RAP'

I wrote the play because it pleased me, and it just happens that I know Irish life best, so I made my methods Irish'.

'Then', I interposed, 'the real truth is you had no idea of catering for the Irish National Theatre. The main idea of the play pleased your own artistic sense, and that you gave it an Irish setting as a mere accident, owing to you intimate knowledge of Irish life'.

'Exactly so,' he answered.

I paused for a moment to reflect upon this new tenet in art. In idealistic quarters it has ever been the cry, art for art's sake; here it was, art for the artist's sake. But though it may seem tall talk on the part of the artist who sets up for himself such a standard, in effect it runs the risk often of being but a poor standard.

'But you know', I suggested, 'the main idea of your play is not a pretty one. You take the worst form of murderer, a parricide, and set

23

him up on a pedestal to be worshipped by the simple, honest people of the West. Is this probable?'

'No, it is not; and it does not matter. Was Don Quixote probable? and still it is art.'

'What was it that at all suggested the main idea of the play?' I asked.

''Tis a thing that really happened. I knew a young fellow in the Arran Islands who had killed his father. And the people befriended him and sent him off to America.'

'But did the girls all make love to him because he had killed his father, and for that only, the sorry-looking, bedraggled, and altogether rebelling figure though he was personally?'

'No. Those girls did not, but mine do.'

'Why do they? What is your idea in making them do it?'

'It is to bring out the humour of the situation. It is a comedy, an extravaganza, made to amuse—'

At this point

THE LIGHTS WENT OUT

and we were left in complete darkness. For the matter of that, I shall always remain in the dark as to Mr. Synge's ideas on art. I am unable either to appreciate them or grasp them.

Mr. Synge and I presently withdrew to the main hall, where the lights were left undisturbed. But here several people got hold of him, and the thread of our conversation was broken for a time.

After some minutes I managed to regain hold of Mr. Synge, when I summed up the case to him:

'Then, I am to understand, Mr. Synge, that your play is not meant to represent Irish life. The fact that a story such as depicted by you actually did happen in a modified way is neither here nor there. Life is not made up of isolated occurrences, but of the things that happen day by day. In fact you had no object whatever in the play except your own art. The plot appealed to your own artistic sense, and for the rest you did not care.'

'Yes', he answered, 'and I don't care a rap how the people take it. I never bother whether my plots are typical Irish or not; but my methods are typical.'

His excitement seemed to go on growing at the interval, to ruffle him still more. He went on talking to me at a rate which made me glad

24

I was not taking him down in shorthand. I cannot believe there is a pencil on earth likely to have kept pace with him then. I was just able to catch him up at the end, to the effect that the speech used by his characters was the actual speech of the people, and that in art a spade must be called a spade.

'But the complaint is, Mr. Synge, that you call it a bloody shovel. Of course I am not speaking from personal experience, for I have not heard a word at all from the stage, though I could not possibly be nearer it. And that reminds me, Mr. Synge, what do you propose to do for the rest of the week, in face of what has taken place to-night?'

'We shall go on with the play to the very end, in spite of all,' he answered, snapping his fingers, more excited than ever. 'I don't care a rap.'[13]

Tuesday night's performance was the scene of even greater excitement;

ABBEY THEATRE SCENES.

MORE UPROAR LAST NIGHT.

MR. SYNGE'S PLAY PRODUCED UNDER POLICE PROTECTION.

INTERRUPTORS ARRESTED.

MR. YEATS' APPEAL FOR A FAIR HEARING.

HUMOROUS EPISODES.

PERFORMANCE CONCLUDES WITH 'GOD SAVE THE KING'.

The attempt to continue the production of 'The Playboy of the Western World' in face of the indignation which accompanied the attempts to stage it on Saturday and Monday evenings, led to further exciting scenes in the Abbey Theatre last night. Up to seven o'clock there was no appearance of any persons near the entrances, but shortly after that hour a number of people began to collect at the pit-door, and at 7:30 there were about forty young men seeking admission through this entrance. Quiet inoffensive young men they appeared to be; but no one could determine, as they waited patiently, if they had come for the purpose of gratifying a curiosity which the newspaper accounts of the previous nights' performances had excited, or with the object of protesting against further production of the insulting play. At this hour also a file of policemen, in the charge of a sergeant, took up a position at the side street, through which the artists entered the Theatre. They were in waiting only for a few minutes when the stage-door opened, and the officers of the law hastily entered. They did not go into the body of the hall, but were evidently held in reserve in the dressingroom. The doors were then opened, and in a short time large numbers had taken their seats in the pit and gallery. At eight o'clock another significant thing happened. A gentleman, stated to be from Galway, entered the hall leading to the stalls, and asked to see Mr. Synge, who promptly made his appearance. The gentleman, having exchanged courtesies with the author, said, turning to a body of young men numbering about twenty, who had assembled in the hall, 'I have brought these supporters,' whereupon the young men were admitted to the stalls, without the formality of purchasing tickets. When they entered the hall, one of them, a gentleman wearing a smart-fitting overcoat, at once flung down a challenge to any man in the pit to fight him. 'Come on, any of you,' he shouted; and immediately came the response, 'We would wipe the streets with you,' followed by a good deal of uproar, and some good-humoured banter at the expense of the overcoated gentleman, whom the audience refused to take seriously. Some of his friends tried to restrain the gentleman's loquacity, but he was apparently determined to make himself heard. His antics were, however, more provocative of mirth than of resentment, and he sat down for a time, and then stood up, shouting.

'I AM A LITTLE BIT DRUNK

and don't know what I am saying.' This confession evoked much amusement. The gentleman then left his seat, and proceeding to the piano in front of the stage, stood up on a chair and bowed in mock courtesy to all parts of the house, after which he sat down and attacked the piano, from which he succeeded in torturing some stray notes of a waltz before he was suppressed by one of the stewards. There were cries of 'Put him out,' whereupon the gallant gentleman, facing the audience, and presenting what he evidently regarded as a heroic figure, shouted defiantly, 'Put me out if you are fit', a challenge which provoked more merriment. Then, as the humour of the situation

26

appeared to have filtered through his turbid intellect, he remarked, 'They won't allow me to speak although I am a labour member,' an observation which was received with laughter.

The orchestra then appeared and played some selections, and at 8:13 Lady Gregory entered and had a conversation with the gentleman from Galway and the overcoated gentleman who expressed his determination to annihilate all opposition. Almost precisely at the same moment, Mr. W. B. Yeats entered the hall by the door leading from the dressing-room, but his appearance was not marked by a demonstration of any kind.

Punctually at 8:15 the curtain was raised, amidst some cheers, on the little one-act tragedy, 'Riders to the Sea', which, like the objectionable play, was also written by Mr. Synge. The piece was performed without any untoward incident marring its production.

At its conclusion, when there was general applause, Mr. Yeats appeared on the stage, and said that a difference of opinion had arisen between the management of the Theatre and some of the audience as to the value of the play which they were now about to produce, and as to the policy of producing it. He did not think that was a moment for more than a little speech, but if any of them wished to discuss the merits of the play, or their right to produce it, he should be delighted to discuss it with them, and answer their comments on some evening when he would come there and debate the matter with any of their opponents. He should then ask them to come up on that platform and address the audience, and he would try and see that they received that fair play which he hoped himself to receive (applause).

A gentleman standing up in the body of the hall said —'I have one word to say; it is this.'

Mr. Yeats—I shall be delighted to hear you in a moment. We have put this play before you to be heard and judged. Every man has a right to hear and condemn it if he pleases, but no man has a right to interfere with another man who wants to hear the play. We shall play on and on, and I assure you our patience will last longer than their patience (applause and groans).

At this stage a number of Trinity College students entered the stalls with the avowed object of suppressing all interruption of the play. The overcoated gentleman then shouted to his friends: 'Come on and have a drink,' and left the hall.

The orchestra played some Irish airs, and at three minutes past nine the curtain rose on 'The Playboy of the Western World.' For a

27

few minutes the opening act was listened to with the deepest silence, and the dialogue between Shawn Keogh and his sweetheart, 'Pegeen Mike', the publican's daughter, evoked some laughter; but shortly afterwards the uproar commenced in the pit, and

A SCENE OF THE GREATEST DISORDER

and excitement ensued. The lights, which had been lowered, were at once turned up, and the famous gentleman in the overcoat, who had returned to the stalls, showed fight, but was held by his friends. Mr. Yeats made a movement as if to restrain the pugnacious spirit of his ardent supporter, but evidently thought his intervention would be ineffectual. Not a word of the play had been heard in the meantime, and after a few minutes the artistes, recognising the hopelessness of making themselves audible above the dreadful din which prevailed, resigned themselves to the inevitable and abandoned even the dumb performance they had been carrying on.

Meantime the gentleman in the overcoat was

SPOILING FOR A ROW,

and one of his friends shouted: 'Let him have the row.' Mr. Synge also tried to restrain him, amidst a perfect hurricane of groans and hisses, hand-clapping and foot-stamping.

After this scene had lasted for some time, Mr. Yeats again got on the stage and asked the audience to remain seated and to listen to the play of a man who, at any rate, was a most distinguished fellow-countryman of theirs (applause, groans, and hisses). Mr. Synge deserved to be heard. If his play was bad, it would die without their help; and if it was good, their hindrances could not impair it either (applause and hisses); but they could impair very greatly the reputation of this country for courtesy and intelligence.

Mr. Yeats then left the stage, amidst renewed cheers, groans, and hisses, above which could be heard bugle notes.

The overcoated gentleman, who had a somewhat racing appearance, stood up and shouted—'Woa,—Woa, you chap there. Woa, be sportsmen.' (groans).

His friends then gathered around the speaker and tried to pull him out of the hall. He resisted violently, and others supported him with the result that chairs were overturned and the excitement wa

28

considerably increased. Finding it impossible to force him out of the hall, persuasion was next resorted to, with the result that in a short time the overcoat was seen to disappear through the stage door, amidst renewed uproar on the part of the occupants of the pit.

Mr. Yeats again ascended the platform and raised his hand for order. He said—We have persuaded one man who was, I regret to say, intoxicated, to leave the meeting. I appeal to all of you who are sober to listen.

A Voice from the Pit—We are all sober here (loud applause).

Meantime the players were standing in a group on the stage, evidently alarmed at the turn affairs were taking, and were evidently discussing the situation amongst themselves.

It was now certain that the occupants of the pit were determined to prevent the performance, and Lady Gregory, Mr. Yeats, Mr. Synge, and a few others held a council as to what steps they would next take. They were apparently unwilling to have resort to police assistance to prevent the expression of popular indignation, but they felt they had to pursue that course or abandon the performance.

After a few minutes Lady Gregory hastily left the hall, and a gentleman in the stall endeavoured to get a hearing with the object of restoring harmony.

'The men who brought me here,' he said, 'are responsible to me, and must give me value for my money.'

A Voice—This is more than a matter of money (loud applause followed by further uproar).

Lady Gregory re-appeared at the stage door, and in a few seconds the police filed in through the same entrance into the body of the hall, amidst renewed groans from the pit. Some of the persons alleged to be responsible for the disturbance were pointed out, and the police, climbing over the chairs into the pit, created a good deal of confusion. In fear of a mêlée a number of ladies left their seats. A gentleman pointed out a young man to the police as causing disorder, and the man was immediately ejected.

At this stage the curtain was lowered, and Mr. Yeats and some of his supporters employed themselves watching people who were making noise, with the object of drawing the attention of the police to them and getting them ejected. They succeeded in getting a number of young men pulled out amidst a terrific uproar, and shouts of 'Where are the militia?'

Inspector Flynn at this stage arrived on the scene with a number of

29

other policemen, whom he stationed at various points with a view of detecting the disturbers, but, nevertheless, the noise continued, but not so loudly as before. However, no attempt was made to resume the performance. Instead the orchestra played some selections, during which there was comparative quiet, but a general feeling of uncertainty prevailed as to what would happen next. After a time the lights were partly lowered, and

AN ATTEMPT WAS MADE TO RESUME THE PLAY,

when the disorder broke out afresh, and in a short time another member of the pit was taken into the custody of the police.

There was a short lull in the storm, during which 'Pegeen Mike' was heard saying to the supposed patricide, 'You are a man who killed your father; then a thousand welcomes to you.' This revolting sentence led to further disorder, and cries of 'That is not life in the West', followed by the most tumultuous uproar. Nothing of the play could be heard except a few disjointed words which conveyed no meaning to the audience. Some cross-firing followed between one of the supporters of the play in the stall and a member of the pit. Shortly afterwards there was another eviction by the police.

One of the lady artistes mentioned the name of an article of female apparel in the course of her dialogue with another of the players, and again the disorder was resumed. Another gentleman was then ejected from the pit and taken into custody. The occupants of the pit were not, however, over awed, but continued stamping their feet, with the result that the play could not be heard. Mr. Yeats was in the meantime wandering about to detect the disturbers and have them ejected.

It was now 10 minutes to 10, and the part of the play had been reached where the publican's daughter was listening admiringly to the recital of Christopher Mahon's account of how he murdered his aged father, when a voice shouted 'Why not get the police to arrest him'. One or two other passages which were heard were also hissed.

A gentleman stood up in the pit and shouted—'They should be beaten off the stage.' (Prolonged applause.)

The appearance of the supposed murderer and the admiration displayed by the village maidens towards him led to increased groaning and hissing.

The curtain was then lowered, and there were further selections

30

from the orchestra. In the interval a number of gentlemen left the stalls.

During the third act the stamping of feet in the pit and occasional outbursts of indignation were pretty constant. Referring to the murder of old Mahon by his son, the publican said, 'It is a hard story,' whereupon a number of the audience aptly remarked, 'It is a rotten story', a remark which was loudly applauded.

The revulsion of feeling on the part of the village people and 'Pegeen Mike' when they discovered that Christopher Mahon was not entitled to be regarded as a hero, as he had not succeeded in murdering his father, caused a further outburst of groans and hisses. The drunken, idotic appearance of the publican returning from a wake was accompanied by expressions of well-merited reprobation.

At this stage (10:20) the gentleman in the overcoat, after an hour's absence, returned to the stalls, and at once made himself heard, and further confusion ensued.

Then one of the artistes said, 'The man that hit his father a clout should have the bravery of ten.' Of course, this revolting sentiment was loudly groaned.

Matters continued in this way until the play concluded. From start to finish not half a dozen consecutive sentences had been heard by the audience.

When the performance came to a close the gentlemen in the stalls who had supported the play sang 'God save the King'.

INTERVIEW WITH MR. W. B. YEATS.

A LECTURE ALL ROUND.

MR. SYNGE'S VERSION OF THE OBJECTIONABLE PASSAGE.

PLAY FOUNED ON LYNCHEHAUN CASE.

Yesterday a representative of the Freeman called at the Abbey Theatre in order to get Mr. Synge's views on the opposition on Saturday night and Monday night to his play, 'The Playboy of the Western World'. He there found that, with Mr. W. B. Yeats, he had gone to lunch in the Metropole Hotel; and here he had a conversation with the two gentlemen on the extraordinary situation that has arisen.

31

Mr. Yeats, who is the Managing Director of the National Theatre Company, thinks 'The Playboy'

and would only discuss it incidentally to what he called the much larger and more important question of the Freedom of the Theatre. His views on this topic are strong, and he expressed them with a good deal of vehemence. Before dealing with this aspect of the business, however, he said that the play had been attacked on the usual grounds of which he thought the people of Dublin had got tired some years ago, and which had nothing whatever to do with art.

ART, AS A FRENCH WRITER HAD SAID,

is 'exaggeration apropos'. Is Lady Macbeth a type of the Queens of Scotland, or Falstaff of the gentlemen of England? Had these critics read 'Bartholomew Fair', by Ben Jonson, the characters in which are all either knaves or fools—are they supposed to be representative of the English people? So far as Mr. Yeats could see

THE PEOPLE WHO FORMED THE OPPOSITION HAD NO BOOKS IN THEIR HOUSES.

All great literature, he added, dealt with exaggerated types, and all tragedy and tragi-comedy with types of sin and folly.

A dramatist is not an historian.

But even, he continued, if the critics were right about the play, that would not make their conduct less than outrageous. A serious issue, said Mr. Yeats, has been rising in Ireland for some time. When

I WAS A LAD, IRISHMEN OBEYED A FEW LEADERS;

but during the last ten years a change has taken place. For leaders we have now societies, clubs, and leagues. Organised opinion of sections and coteries has been put in place of these leaders, one or two of whom were men of genius. Instead of a Parnell, a Stephens, or a Butt, we must obey the demands of commonplace and ignorant people, who try to take on an appearance of strength by imposing some crude shibboleth on their own and others' necks. They do not persuade,

32

for that is difficult; they do not expound, for that needs knowledge. There are some exceptions, as heretofore, but the mass only understand conversion by

TERROR, THREATS, AND ABUSE.

You think the opposition last night represented this school of criticism?

Yes. The forty and odd young men who came down last night, not to judge the play, but to prevent other people from doing so, merely carried out a method which is becoming general in our national affairs. There have been

SEVERAL OF THESE ATTACKS ON THEATRES OF LATE,

and it is nothing to the point that the attacks have not hitherto been on plays of serious purpose. Much they have attacked has been as bad as they thought it, but that is nothing to the issue. When they are in the right they strike at the freedom of their country just as decisively. They have been so long in

MENTAL SERVITUDE

that they cannot understand life if their head is not in some bag. What does it matter whether it is a policeman or a club secretary who holds the string?

Of course we are going on with the play, said Mr. Yeats. We will go on until the play has been heard, and heard sufficiently to be judged on its merits. We had only announced its production for one week. We have now decided to play all next week as well, if the opposition continue, with the exception of one night, when

I SHALL LECTURE ON THE FREEDOM OF THE THEATRE,

and invite our opponents to speak on its slavery to the mob if they have a mind to.

Anyone, said Mr. Yeats, who writes that he has not been able to hear shall be sent a free ticket; and we

SHALL GO ON THUS AS LONG AS THERE IS ONE MAN

who has wanted to hear the play and has been prevented by noise.

33

At this point Mr. Synge remarked that that might mean giving free tickets to the opposition.

That can't be helped, said Mr. Yeats. If our critics wish to make liars of themselves it is not our affair.

In the Abbey Theatre, he added, the artists will always call the tune. And he made the point that there was

ONE PERSON AT LEAST WHO WOULD COME THE GAINER

out of this tumult—it would, no doubt, sell an extra edition of Mr. Synge's book.

MR. SYNGE, ASKED ABOUT THE WORD WHICH CAUSED THE UPROAR
ON SATURDAY NIGHT

towards the close of the play, said it was an everyday word in the West of Ireland, which would not be taken offence at there, and might be taken differently by people in Dublin. It was used without any objection in Douglas Hyde's 'Songs of Connaught', in the Irish, but what could be published in Irish perhaps could not be published in English?

On the question of the main point of the play, Mr. Synge repeated Mr. Yeats' idea about art being exaggerated, and said that as a fact

THE IDEA OF THE PLAY WAS SUGGESTED TO HIM

by the fact that a few years ago a man who committed a murder was kept hidden by the people on one of the Arran Islands until he could get off to America, and also by the case of Lynchehaun, who was a most brutal murderer of a woman, and yet, by the aid of Irish peasant women, managed to conceal himself from the police for months, and to get away also.[14]

The Freeman's Journal *could not resist answering one of Yeats' arguments; in an unsigned article in the same issue, it comments:*

Mr. Yeats asks is Lady Macbeth a type of the Queens of Scotland? The question is puerile. It might have some relevance if Lady Macbeth danced a Highland fling after the murder of Duncan, and if she was congratulated all round on the murder.

34

Both the defenders of the play and those opposed to it were accused of employing claques, and whether they were actually paid or not, two vocal and even violent groups of young men prevented the audience from hearing much of the play's dialogue. Against this obstruction the Irish Times *protests:*

The National Theatre Company cannot complain that Dublin's reception of Mr. Synge's play, 'The Playboy of the Western World', at the Abbey Theatre has been lacking in warmth. The play, Mr. Synge tells us, was 'made to amuse'. Perhaps a section of our countrymen can only achieve amusement by working themselves into a violent passion. At any rate they have amused themselves during the last nights by making such a pandemonium at the Abbey Theatre that the actors have been obliged to go through their parts in dumb show. The charges made against the play in defense of this rowdy conduct are that its plot and characters are an outrageous insult to the West of Ireland and its people, and that some of its language is vulgar, and even indelicate. The hero of the play is a disreputable tramp, who only ceases to be courted by the women of a Western village when they discover that he is not really a parricide. Such an incident would be uncommon in any civilised country. The 'Irish Ireland' critics of Mr. Synge's play have decided that it would be absolutely impossible in Ireland—just as they decided previously, in the case of the 'Countess Cathleen', that it would be impossible for any Irishwoman to sell her soul to the devil, and, in the case of 'The Spell', that it would be impossible for any Irishwoman to believe in the potency of a love-philtre. 'Calumny gone raving mad' is how the *Freeman's Journal* describes 'The Playboy of the Western World', and during the last two nights considerable bodies of apparently intelligent young men have endorsed that verdict to go raving mad at the Abbey Theatre.

It need hardly be said that no well-balanced mind can defend for a single moment the *Sinn Fein* party's crude and violent methods of dramatic criticism. Let us admit at once that Mr. Synge's play has serious faults. It seems to be granted by his most enthusiastic admirers that some of his language has the material fault of being indelicate and the artistic fault of obscuring the essential realities of the play. An error in taste, however, is not a crime, and the shriekings of an infuriated mob are not the proper method of rebuking it. As to the main incident of the play being impossible, Mr. Synge has produced *prima facie* evidence in favour of its possibility. The idea, he says, was sug-

35

gested to him by the fact that a few years ago a man who committed a murder was kept hidden by the people on one of the Arran Islands until he could get off to America. Mr. Synge refers us also to the case of Lynchehaun, who was a most brutal murderer of a woman, and yet, by the aid of Irish peasant women, managed to conceal himself from the police for months. The fact is that while, in our opinion, there are aspects of Mr. Synge's play which may be justly and severely criticised, the *Sinn Fein* shouters have ignored these altogether, and have founded their objections on a theory of Celtic impeccability which is absurd in principle, and intolerable, when it is sought to be rigidly imposed as a canon of art. Our own criticism of the play is based solely on artistic considerations. We blame Mr. Synge, for instance, for not having made his motive clear to his audience. Hardly any member of the gathering which witnessed the first production on Saturday night seems to have been able to guess what the author was 'driving at'. In another column that clever writer, 'Pat', evolves an interesting and plausible theory of what was in Mr. Synge's mind. Even, however, if it were a true theory Mr. Synge appears to have failed to give his audience a definite appreciation of it. But, if Mr. Synge is correctly represented in an 'interview' which he gave yesterday to an evening newspaper, 'Pat's' motive was not really his motive —in fact, he had no serious motive at all. He is said to have stated that the play is an extravaganza, that he wrote it to please himself, and that its Irish setting was a mere accident. If this be a true explanation we confess that we find it hard to defend 'The Playboy of the Western World'. The idle aim of a mere extravaganza does not justify the grimly realistic treatment of a distinctly unpleasant theme. A serious purpose, clearly brought home, would have vindicated the play. If, however, Mr. Synge was simply a humourist, then he has played with edged tools, and he can hardly lay claim to that feeling of self-approval which was the consolation of the Roman actress when she, too, was hissed from the stage.

Yet even if the faults of Mr. Synge's play were much greater than we take them to be, the treatment which it has received from a section of the public is utterly indefensible. Mr. Synge is an artist, and, as such, not immune from criticism. The claim—not now advocated for the first time—that people should be allowed to howl down a play or a book merely because it offends their crude notions of patriotism cannot be tolerated for a moment, if there is ever to be any such thing as independent thought in Ireland. We heartily endorse everything that

Mr. W. B. Yeats said yesterday on this subject. . . . It is high time for thoughtful Irishmen of all parties to make a stand for freedom of thought and speech against bodies which seek to introduce into the world of the mind the methods which the Western branches of the United Irish League have introduced into politics. For this reason we sympathise with the plucky stand which the National Theatre Company is making against the organised tyranny of the clap-trap patriots. We hope, however, that the next battle will be over a play to which, as a work of art, we shall be able to give a more whole-hearted approval than we find it possible to offer to 'The Playboy of the Western World'.[15]

The most substantial, albeit partial, review of the play in Dublin dailies is of 'Pat' (Patrick Kenny) in the Irish Times:

THAT DREADFUL PLAY
(BY PAT.)

Dublin audiences are said to be very critical, and those at the Abbey Theatre are said to be the most critical of them, but they have not yet permitted themselves to see 'The Playboy of the Western World', and I hope the plucky players will play on until there is a chance to understand, when the screaming has exhausted itself. The screamers do not know what they are missing.

In a way there are two plays, one within another, and unless the inner one is seen, I am not surprised at the screaming about the outer one, which in itself is repellent, and must so remain until seen in the light of the conception out of which it arises, as when we welcome a profane quotation in a sermon, recognising a higher purpose that it is employed to emphasise. 'The Playboy of the Western World' is a highly moral play, deriving its motive from sources as pure and as lofty as the externals of its setting are necessarily wild and vulgar; and I cannot but admire the moral courage of the man who has shot his dreadful searchlight into our cherished accumulation of social skeletons. He has led our vision through the Abbey street stage into the heart of Connaught, and revealed to us there truly terrible truths, of our own making, which we dare not face for the present. The merciless accuracy of his revelation is more than we can bear. Our eyes tremble at it. The words chosen are, like the things they express, direct and dreadful, by themselves intolerable to conventional taste, yet full of vital beauty in their truth to the conditions of life, to the

37

character they depict, and to the sympathies they suggest. It is as if we looked in a mirror for the first time, and found ourselves hideous. We fear to face the thing. We shrink at the word for it. We scream.

True, a play ought to explain itself; but then, the audience has not yet permitted it to explain itself. Perhaps the externals are unworkably true to the inherent facts of life behind them; but that is a superficial matter, and though it is hard for an artist to select language less strong than the truth impelling him, I think a working modification may be arrived at without scarificing anything essential. Mr. Synge must remember that the shock was sincere.

'Pegeen' is a lively peasant girl in her father's publichouse on the wild wayside by the Western sea, and it is arranged for her to marry 'Shaneen Keogh,' the half idiot, who has a farm, but not enough intelligence to cut his yellow hair. There is no love. Who could think of loving 'Shaneen'? Love could not occur to her through him. He has not enough intelligence to love. He has not enough character to have a single vice in him, and his only apparent virtue is a trembling terror of 'Father Reilly'. Yet there is nothing unusual in the marriage of such a girl to such a person, and it does not occur to her that love ought to have anything to do with the matter.

Why is 'Pegeen' prepared to marry him? 'God made him; therefore, let him pass for a man', and in all his unfitness, he is the fittest available! Why? Because the fit ones have fled. He remains because of his cowardice and his idiocy in a region where fear is the first of the virtues, and where the survival of the unfittest is the established law of life. Had he been capable, he would have fled. His lack of character enables him to accept the conditions of his existence, where more character could but make him less acceptable, and therefore, less happy. Character wants freedom, and so escapes, but the 'Shaneens' remain to reproduce themselves in the social scheme. We see in him how the Irish race die out in Ireland, filling the lunatic asylums more full from a declining population, and selecting for continuance in the future the human specimens most calculated to bring the race lower and lower. 'Shaneen' shows us why Ireland dies while the races around us prosper faster and faster. A woman is interested in the nearest thing to a man that she can find within her reach, and that is why 'Pegeen' is prepared to marry her half idiot with the yellow hair. 'Shaneen' accepts terror as the regular condition of his existence, and so there is no need for him to emigrate with the strong and clever ones who insist on freedom for their lives.

38

Such is the situation into which the 'Playboy' drifts, confessing in callous calmness that he has killed his father, and claiming sanctuary as pot boy in the publichouse—not, by the way, a convincing position in which to disguise a murderer. Women do not choose murderers for their husbands, but the 'Playboy' is a real, live man, and the only other choice is the trembling idiot, who would be incapable even to kill his father. Instinctively and immediately, 'Pegeen' prefers the murderer. Besides, there is the story of why he 'stretched his father with the loy'. The father had wanted to force him into a marriage with a woman he hated. The son had protested. The father had raised the scythe, but the son's blow with the spade had fallen first. Murder is not pleasant, but what of the other crime—that of a father forcing his son to marry a woman he hated? Were it not for this crime, the other could not have followed. A real, live man was new and fascinating to 'Pegeen', even a parricide, and the man who had killed his father, rather than marry a woman he hated, might at least be capable of loving sincerely. Then, he was a man who had achieved something, if only murder, and he had achieved the murder obviously because his better character had not been permitted to govern him. When trembling idiocy tends to be the standard of life, intelligence and courage can easily become critical, and women do not like trembling men. In their hearts, they prefer murderers. What is a woman to do in conditions of existence that leave her a choice only between the cowardly fool and the courageous criminal?

The choice itself is full of drama, the more tragic because it is the lot of a community. The woman's only alternatives are to be derilect or to be degraded; poor 'Pegeen' personifies a nation in which the 'Shaneens' prevail, and in which strong, healthy men can stay only to be at war with their surroundings. It is the revolt of Human Nature against the terrors ever inflicted on it in Connacht, and in some subtle way of his own the dramatist has succeeded in realising the distinction; so that even when the guilt is confessed, we cannot accept 'The Playboy' quite as a murderer, and we are driven back to the influences of his environment, for the origin of his responsibility, feeling that if we do not permit men to grow morally, we are ourselves to blame for the acts by which they shock us. Such are Synge's insights into life and character in Connacht. Can the Western peasantry have a truer friend than the one who exhibits to criticism and to condemnation the forces afflicting their lives?

The peasant women of Connacht are no more partial to murderers than other women in other countries, but we must take the conduct of women anywhere in the light of their environment, and we must take the conduct of men in the same way. The difference between a hero and a murderer is sometimes, in the comparative numbers they have killed, morally in favour of the murderer; and we all know how the 'pale young curate' loses his drawingroom popularity when the unmarried subaltern returns from his professional blood-spilling. It is not that women love murder; it is that they hate cowardice, and in 'Pegeen's' world it is hard for a man to be much better than a coward. Hence the half-idiot with the yellow hair, who, controlling his share of the nation's land, can inflict his kind on the community generation after generation.

The fierce truth and intensity of the dramatist's insight make strength of expression inevitable, but, confining myself strictly to the artistic interest, I feel that the language is overdone, and that the realism is overdone. They irritate, and, worse still, they are piled up to such excess in the subsidiaries of expression as to make us lose sight in some measure of the dramatic essentials. As to the discussions on feminine underclothing, I have often heard discussions more familiar among the peasantry themselves, without the remotest suggestion of immorality, and if Dublin is shocked in this connection, it is because its mind is less clean than that of the Connacht peasant women.

It itself, the plot is singularly undramatic by construction, suggesting drama rather than exploiting 'cheap' effect. We have to think down along the shafts of light into Connacht in order to realise the picture at the end of the vista, but when we see it we find it inevitable and fascinating. The play is more a psychological revelation than a dramatic process, but it is both.

I have not said much to suggest 'comedy', which is the official adjective for this play. I have tried to bring out the unseen interests that await criticism and appreciation while the Abbey street audiences scream. It is a play on which many articles could be written.

There was a large audience last night, mainly there to 'boo', but they must pay to come in, so that the management stands to make money, and to be heard in the end.[16]

Prompted by this review, Synge wrote to The Irish Times *one of the few statements of his intentions and dramatic theories:*

SIR,—As a rule the less a writer says about his own work the better, but as my views have been rather misunderstood in an interview which appeared in one of the evening papers, and was alluded to in your leader today, I would like to say a word or two to put myself right. The interview took place in conditions that made it nearly impossible for me—in spite of the patience and courtesy of the interviewer—to give a clear account of my views about the play, and the lines I followed in writing it. 'The Playboy of the Western World' is not a play with 'a purpose' in the modern sense of the word, but although parts of it are, or are meant to be, extravagant comedy, still a great deal that is in it, and a great deal more that is behind it, is perfectly serious, when looked at in a certain light. That is often the case, I think, with comedy, and no one is quite sure to-day whether 'Shylock' and 'Alceste' should be played seriously or not. There are, it may be hinted, several sides to 'The Playboy'.

'Pat', I am glad to notice, has seen some of them in his own way. There may be still others if anyone cares to look for them. Yours, etc.

J. M. SYNGE.[17]

But all appeals to restraint went unheeded. The Freeman's Journal *remained adamant in its insistence that the play should not be continued; the theatre's refusal to give in to the protestors just proved it was not the national theatre it had paraded as:*

Surely the managers of the Abbey Theatre have by this time had enough of their police-protected drama. Mr. Yeats prophesied that his friend Mr. Synge would profit by the popular condemnation of his play through the sale of his book. In that fashion the repulsive calumny can be brought to the knowledge of all who are anxious to read it without the scandal of its public performance in Dublin. The pecuniary profit, which is regarded as so important, might be further increased, if, as we have suggested, a bargain could be struck with Mr. Long for the use of the book in his forthcoming anti-Irish crusade. There is all the less reason for brazening out the attempt to inflict it further on an audience in Dublin. All the fine talk about preserving or restoring the national spirit by literary inspiration finds its outcome in disgusting travesties of Irish life and character like 'The Playboy'. A correspondent shrewdly suggests that there never would have been an Abbey National Theatre founded if the little knot of decadents who exploit it for the profitable disposal of their literary wares had been able to find a market elsewhere. Certainly no love of Ireland, and no

41

sympathy with her national spirit, was responsible for 'The Playboy'. It is not a little curious to find that, in the estimation of the managers of the Abbey street house, the true function of a National Theatre is to slander the nation.[18]

Wednesday night's performance was no more successful than those of previous nights:

Before the doors of the Abbey Theatre were opened last night the building and its vicinity presented a somewhat singular appearance. Large crowds were assembled in the streets, the entrances to the popular parts of the house were literally besieged by hundreds of people. Police were on duty at every available point, whilst a strong contingent of constables were admitted into the structure by the stage door. In a few minutes after the time appointed for the admission of the public the theatre was thronged to excess—never before had its holding capacity been so severely tested.

The pit and gallery were filled with gentlemen who regarded 'The Playboy' as an insult to Ireland. In the stalls were unquestionably many persons, including Trinity College students, who looked at it from a totally different standpoint. Unlike the two previous evenings when the expressions of dissent were not heard until Mr. Synge's so-called comedy was present, the house immediately resounded with boos, hisses, and such like noises. It appeared as if there was

GOING TO BE PRETTY HOT WORK.

To add to the clamour, a gentleman stood up in the gallery and began to speak. He said that they were assembled there to protest against immorality on the Irish Stage, and would put down immorality in that theatre. With that protest he would retire, although he had paid for his seat. Immediately afterwards he stated that he had changed his mind and would remain. He, however, did not do so, as he was soon afterwards ejected. But he was evidently irrepressible. He quickly reappeared in the stalls, and was proceeding to thank the audience for the cordial reception they had accorded him, when once more he was what is termed 'shown the door'.

Mr. Synge at this stage entered the theatre. A storm of hisses, boos, and uncomplimentary epithets greeted him. There were also cries of 'Take off your hat. Have manners.' 'Tramp, tramp, the Boys are Marching', was then sung vigorously.

Amid the tumult the curtain was raised on the inaugural piece, 'Riders to the Sea'. This piteous one-act tragedy never had a more sympathetic audience. Silence reigned throughout the house during its presentation—at the close fervid plaudits rendered the raising of the curtain inevitable.

A rather ominous incident took place almost immediately.

POLICE HAD BEEN SEEN IN THE WINGS.

About a dozen constables now took up positions on each side of the pit, whilst others marched into the gallery. Outbursts of indignation greeted the manoeuvre.

At last the tug-of-war began—the performance of 'The Playboy of the Western World'. As usual, the first ten minutes passed off quietly— in fact there was a fair share of applause. However, affairs changed when the self-accused parricide was received with open arms by the peasants, both masculine and feminine. Shouts of 'Get out' were hurled from all directions, whilst cat-calls, strident bugle notes, and fierce denunciations added to the terrific din. But, on the other hand, there were shouts of 'Order', and 'Fair Play'. For fully five minutes not a word spoken on the stage could be heard; but from that to the end of the act the dialogue, although the interruptions continued, was not completely smothered, as was the case on Monday and Tuesday nights. An almost similar condition of affairs existed in connection with the remaining two sections of the drama. There were numerous shouts of 'That's not the West of Ireland'. The wooing by Widow Quin of 'The Playboy' gave rise to a demonstration of marked hostility. Just as the curtain was descending on the act Mr. Yeats and Mr. Synge came into the stalls—they were vehemently hissed, but were also cheered.

The second act was inaugurated with much excitement. Hisses were freely indulged in, as also were ejaculations of 'Give them a chance'. The bestowal of presents on 'The Playboy' because he was a man who

43

had killed his father awoke yells of execration. Not a word was heard for some minutes. The mention of a certain article of ladies' apparel also raised a storm of indignation, amongst which were sturdy vociferations of 'Shut up. We have heard enough'. This was quickly followed, in reference to one of the characters, by derisive shouts of

'SEND THE BOBBIES TO HIM'—'CALL THE POLICEMEN',

to which a voice replied, 'There's no necessity—the house is full of them'. The act concluded amidst a hurricane of uproar. To while away the interval the majority of the audience commenced whistling, in every conceivable note, 'The Peeler and the Goat'. This was varied by an unexpected interlude.

A low-sized Englishman in the stalls, who was an upholder of the play, got into an altercation with a young gentleman in the pit who entertained diametrically opposite views. At length, the former challenged the latter to fight him. The gage of battle was at once taken up. Followed by a couple of hundred persons the combatants made their way into the vestibule. Here

SEVERAL BLOWS WERE EXCHANGED.

An animated scene ensued—there was considerable singing and commotion—no one could exactly say how the incident terminated.

The third and last act was now ushered in. Almost at its commencement one of the characters declares, 'There will be right sport before nightfall'. This was so very apropos to the exciting situation that all parties in the theatre joined in an outburst of hearty laughter. But a change promptly came over the scene. Accordingly, as phrases or sentiments were uttered which the demonstrants deemed objectionable an inferno of yells, hisses, and bugle calls held sway, during which the police forcibly ejected several of the interrupters. Thus ended the fourth performance of 'The Playboy of the Western World', a portion of the original text of which has apparently been altered or excised.

But the audience did not seem inclined to leave the theatre on the conclusion of the play. There were ironical cries of 'Author' and 'A speech'. These were not responded to. Matters appeared rather critical. A number of gentlemen began to address knots of admirers. Mr. Monahan, a prominent Sinn Feiner, mounted a seat and denounced the piece, saying he had never seen or heard anything like

44

it. His discourse was cut short by policemen, who insisted on him leaving the building. This apparently was the signal for general action on the part of the constables, who proceeded to clear the gallery.

The night's work was, however, not over. The rival sections marched through Abbey street, O'Connell street, and other thoroughfares giving vent to the faith that was in them. They were followed by strong detachments of police, whilst other bodies of the force were stationed at points of 'vantage. So far as could be ascertained, no serious disturbance occurred.

Mr. Synge, in reply to a Freeman representative last night, said—'My policy is unchanged'.

*   *   *

THE SCENE AT THE THEATRE.

by one of

THE EJECTED.

I have been asked as one of those who was ejected from the Abbey Theatre on Tuesday night, to pen a description of my experience; yet I confess I feel little zest in doing so. I am not one of those who take a mean delight in the degradation of

THINGS THAT ONCE PROMISED NOBLY;

and I, who welcomed and supported the Abbey Theatre while it followed the counsel of wisdom feel nothing but pity for the contempt-ible bedraggled position which it occupies to-day. I can feel no pleasure in seeing Mr. W. B. Yeats, once a patriot and still a poet, prosecuting men in the Police Courts for

HOOTING A BAD PLAY

at his theatre. Why it is a better tragi-comedy than anything that could be conceived in the grotesquest fancies of the clever comic writers of his foredoomed theatre. How Moliere would have expanded on the spectacle of our dreamy poet swearing in the Northern Police

45

Court that he distinctly heard a boo! What a spectacle for gods and men, the

CHAMPION OF A FREE IRISH THEATRE

calling in the police, and admitting drunken anti-Irish rowdies to the stalls free for the purpose of supporting what those rowdies welcomed with delight as giving an unfavourable picture of their countrymen. What an instance of National topsy-turveydom in the picture of this Irish dramatist, this authority on the ways and speech of the Western peasant

STANDING SICK, SILENT, AND ASHAMED

when addressed in Irish.

There is no pleasure in kicking a dead dog, especially if when alive we thought well of it; and the Abbey Theatre is now dead and rotten as a National Theatre. The pictures which I saw on Tuesday night make clear the absolute impossibility of the 'Abbey' being ever accepted by the people of Ireland as a National institution of theirs. I saw a number of

DRUNKEN TRINITY STUDENTS

standing in the stalls, brandishing their sticks and inviting fight. I saw seated facing the stage a number of respectable young men who were certainly not making as much noise as the supporters of the play, who were quite sober, and who, I am absolutely satisfied (for I was among them) were

NOT AN 'ORGANISED GANG',

but individual Irishmen inspired by much the same feelings that prompted the outburst in Liverpool a month ago.

I saw Mr. Yeats going round with the police and pointing out men to them. I saw him give two Irish-speaking gentlemen in charge and accompany them to the station. This last picture was the most pitiful of all. Mr. Yeats looked as if he was thoroughly ashamed of himself, yet was determined to brazen out his false position.

46

The crowning spectacle of this tragi-comedy was the sight of a

CORDON OF POLICE SURROUNDING THE ABBEY THEATRE

to protect it from the people; and as I went home I said to myself with a sigh, 'Thus ends the "National" Theatre of Ireland.'[19]

The trials of some of those arrested provided an added scene of excitement:

POLICE PROSECUTIONS.

INTERRUPTERS CHARGED.

MR. W. B. YEATS EXAMINED.

HEAVY PENALTIES.

Yesterday in the Northern Police Court, before Mr. Mahony, Patrick Columb, 30 Chelmsford road, clerk, was charged by Constables 47C, 87C, and 113D with 'being guilty of offensive behaviour in the pit of the Abbey Theatre between 10 and 11 o'clock on the previous night on the occasion of the production of a play styled "The Playboy of the Western World" there, by shouting, hissing, and booing and stamping his feet, and with, when spoken to by the constables, using obscene language to the annoyance of the audience'.

Mr. Tobias appeared for the police.

Mr. Lidwell defended. Mr. M'Cune, solicitor, watched the case for the Abbey Theatre Company.

Police-Constable 47C, in reply to Mr. Tobias, deposed that he was on duty in the Abbey Theatre on Tuesday when the disturbance occurred. It commenced between 10 and 11 o'clock at the performance of the play. He

SAW THE DEFENDANT STAMPING HIS FEET,

and heard him boohing and hissing.

Did this cause disturbance and annoyance to the audience? Yes; and some of them called 'Hush'. A number of others also caused disturbance.

Did the defendant say anything? Yes, when I put my hand on him he said, 'Who are you, you—?' He refused to stop creating the noise.

Cross-examined by Mr. Lidwell—I went into the theatre at about twenty minutes to ten o'clock. There was great noise in the place. We were called in

TO QUELL THE DISTURBANCE.

Some of the audience wanted to hear the play and some did not.

Did you hear any offensive word used on the stage? Yes, I did. I heard one offensive word.

As offensive as anything said amongst the audience?

Witness smiled, but did not reply.

Police-Constable 87C, examined by Mr. Tobias, said he was called into the theatre at about twenty minutes to ten o'clock. He heard the defendant hissing and booing, and saw him stamping his feet. Some of the audience asked to have the defendant put out. Witness heard Constable 47C caution the defendant, and the latter used an offensive expression loudly and within the hearing of the audience.

Constable 113D was also examined. He said, in reply to Mr. Tobias, that there was a great deal of noise. The majority of the people in the pit were hissing and booing.

Were they doing anything else? Yes; whistling and stamping the floor. The people in the stalls were calling for order. The defendant was in the pit, and he heard him use an offensive expression to 47C.

Cross-examined by Mr. Lidwell—There was a general tumult.

I COULDN'T HEAR ANYTHING ON THE STAGE

owing to the noise.

MR. YEATS EXAMINED.

Mr. William B. Yeats, examined by Mr. Tobias, said—I am managing director of the Abbey Theatre. I was there last night when a play called 'The Playboy of the Western World' was performed. From the first rising of the curtain there was an obviously organised attempt to prevent the play being heard. That was from a section of the pit. The stalls and balcony were anxious to hear the play. The noise consisted of shouting and booing and stamping of feet. I did not hear six

48

consecutive lines of the play last night owing to the noise. The section that caused the disturbance was not part of the regular audience. The conduct of the section was riotous and offensive,

AND DISTURBED AND ANNOYED THE AUDIENCE.

Cross-examined by Mr. Lidwell—We have a patent for this theatre. Did you read this play? Yes, and passed it.

Is it a caricature of the Irish people? It is no more a caricature of the people of Ireland than 'Macbeth' is a caricature of the people of Scotland or 'Falstaff' a caricature of the gentlemen of England. The play is

AN EXAMPLE OF THE EXAGGERATION OF ART.

I have not the slightest doubt but that we shall have more of these disturbances.

Mr. Lidwell—Is the play typical of the Irish people? No; it is an exaggeration.

Then you admit it is a caricature? An exaggeration.

Mr. Mahony said he was satisfied that the defendant had been guilty of disorderly behaviour, and ordered him to pay a fine of 40s, with the alternative of one month's imprisonment, and to find sureties in £10 for his future good behaviour.

A SECOND CHARGE.

Piaraos Beaslaoi, aged 25, was charged by Constables 170C and 121C with a like offence in the same theatre.

Police-Constable 170C, examined by Mr. Tobias, said he was on duty at the theatre from twenty minutes to 8 p.m. There was booing and shouting and stamping continuously from about 9 o'clock. It was principally in the pit. The noise

PREVENTED ANYONE HEARING WHAT WENT ON ON THE STAGE.

He saw the defendant in the pit, and he was booing and hissing. He heard one section cry, 'Put him out'. He spoke to the defendant at twenty minutes to ten o'clock and arrested him.

49

when he made the arrest.

Police-Constable 121C gave similar evidence.

Mr. W. B. Yeats deposed—I saw the defendant at the performance last night in the Abbey Theatre. There was an organised disturbance by a section of the pit to prevent the play being heard. He saw the defendant arrested, and saw him before the arrest rise up and yell at the top of his voice.

Mr. Mahony—Did he say anything?

Witness—He addressed some words to me in Irish.

Mr. Mahony—Were they complimentary or the reverse?

Witness—I am sorry to say

I UNDERSTAND NO IRISH.

Mr. Mahony—Well, I know some Irish, and I know that one can say very scathing things in Irish.

The Defendant—If your worship had been present you would have heard nothing unedifying from me.

This closed the case for the prosecution.

Mr. Mahony—Now, Mr. Beaslaoi, what have you to say?

Mr. Beaslaoi stated that he was no member of any organised gang who went to the theatre for the purpose of objecting. He went with two friends, and did not know the other objectors, and his blood boiled at the attempt to coerce public opinion. The men in the stalls were standing up and shaking their sticks. Mr. Yeats stood over him and said he would give in charge the next man who 'booed'. Just then a particularly objectionable expression was used on the stage, and he (the defendant), in common with a number of others, 'booed'. Mr. Yeats then pointed him out to the constable, and he was taken in charge. He was satisfied with the result, and no threats or penalties would deter him from objecting to what he considered an outrage on the Irish people. Previous to this he had been an admirer of the Abbey Theatre and a regular supporter of it.

Mr. Mahony said this was a different case from the last.

The Defendant—I have made my protest I consider

EVERY TRUE IRISHMAN WOULD ACT IN THE SAME WAY.

Mr. Mahony—You are entitled to indulge in legitimate criticism and also in a reasonable form of disapproval, but you are not entitled to be guilty of such behaviour as would be offensive to other persons in the play and prevent their performance. He understood the defendant to be an enthusiast in Celtic matters. He did not want to be too severe on him if he would give an undertaking that he would not take any part in these disturbances again.

Mr. Yeats said he would be satisfied with such an understanding. Defendant said

HE WOULD MAKE NO APPEAL TO MR. YEATS,

but wished him to push the matter to the utmost extremity. They would then have the spectacle of a man brought into the Police Court for making a protest against

AN OUTRAGE ON IRISH NATIONALITY.

Mr. Mahony—A protest which the law does not permit. Surely you can make a protest without breaking the law.

The Defendant—Mr. Yeats pointed me out to the police and is responsible for this prosecution.

Mr. Mahony—I must fine you 40s., or in default, a month's imprisonment, and I will take your own sureties for good behaviour.[20]

Note that the accusations of the disturbance being organized were never proven. In the case of another young man brought to trial the following day, the magistrate, Mr. Wall, defined the precedents in handling such a case, and inserted his own reactions to the present situation:

Mr. Wall, proceeding to deal with the case, quoted a decision given by a former Lord Chief Justice, Bushe, in a similar case which came before him, a judge as to whose worth all creeds and sections of the people of his time agreed. That judge had said that the rights of an audience in a theatre were very well defined. They might cry down a play which they disliked, or hiss and booh the actors who depended for their positions on the good-will of audiences, but they must not act in such a manner as had a tendency to excite uproar or disturbance. Their censure or approbation, though they might be noisy in expressing it, must not be riotous, and must be the expression of the

51

feeling of the moment. If premeditated by a number of persons com-
bined beforehand to cry down a performance or an actor it became
criminal. That is the opinion of one of the most respected lights of
the legal Bench. Mr. Wall next referred to a judgment of Lord Justice
Venston, giving effect to a similar view as to the rights of

THEATRE AUDIENCES.

So far as he knew, no such privilege as was attached to a theatre was
recognised in regard to other places of amusement. A theatre was on
different grounds. The theatre in Ireland had always been supposed
to be in olden times the resort of people who sought interest, culture,
and instruction, and they expected to get these, and not to have their
people lampooned and reviled. If this young man had been guilty of
any special individual misconduct it would, of course, be a proper
case for summary jurisdiction, but in this case the young man appeared
to have been exercising his privilege, although the Inspector had acted
perfectly right in the discharge of his duty in trying to put down the
row which was going on. It was lamentable that the parties who were
responsible for this most regrettable condition of affairs were not
brought to book. On the other hand it might be

WELL TO CONSIDER

on the part of the Crown whether those who persisted in bringing
forward theatrical procedure of such a character as to excite popular
odium and opposition, and which could not be tolerated at all events
in Ireland, where practically there were two worlds, one wishing to
be at the throat of the other, and one wishing to avoid what the other
wished to intrude—whether those who were responsible for that
should not themselves be brought forward. He did not think the
defendant's conduct was any worse than the conduct of the others
who differed from him. Why the case was tried as a riot he did not
know. It was a melancholy thing, Mr. Wall went on to say, that in an
institution which he understood was provided for the popular view of
the Irish drama, there should have been caused all that appeared to
have happened

DURING THE PAST WEEK

and that matters should have been put forward on the stage that

52

great numbers of the Irish people resented. That, he said, was a strange complication of theatrical matter for the amusement of the Irish people. However, this was only by the way. On the whole, he must convict the defendant, although he did not consider it a case for serious punishment.[21]

Padraic Colum, whose father was one of those arrested and found guilty, published one of the most sensible appraisals of the situation which was already approaching the absurd:

TO THE EDITOR OF THE FREEMAN'S JOURNAL

SIR,—The organised attempt to prevent a hearing for 'The Playboy of the Western World' is bound to produce more serious results on Irish life than if the opinions expressed in that play were circulated freely. We should beware of bringing violence into the places of the intellect. That a man should be allowed free speech in public is a paradox, but it is a paradox that everyone who values thought should be eager to defend. An organised opposition to a play is very unfair in many ways. It is unfair to those who wish to hear the play; it is unfair to the actors—actors are peculiarly sensitive to demonstration, and they are not primarily responsible for the opinions expressed in the play.

On the other hand, the management of the Abbey Theatre have made a grave tactical mistake in introducing police into the theatre. It was a mistake to associate a theatre whose effort is to become a National theatre with police protection. It was a risk to subject an audience to the ordeal of the police. If an arrest is to be made, a Dublin policeman will inevitably go for the mildest man who happens to make himself conspicuous. Last night my father was arrested in the Abbey Theatre. This morning he was required to find surety for £20, as the management of the theatre expected a renewal of the opposition. Nothing could be more unjust. My father is, to a certain extent, a student of the drama. He is genuinely interested in the attempt to create a National drama. He certainly went to the Abbey Theatre to hear Mr. Synge's play. He is not in sympathy with an organised opposition. As a matter of fact, he has friends in the present National Theatre Society. He disapproved of certain passages in Mr. Synge's play, and expressed his disapproval. When a policeman interfered he used a strong expression, the expression that a man in an excited

53

crowd would be likely to use. For this he was brought before a magistrate this morning, and treated as a member of a gang. The management of the Abbey Theatre have frankly used intimidation against intimidation, and this piece of injustice is one of the results.

The opposition to 'The Playboy of the Western World' has only prevented a sane estimate of the play. Many people interested in Irish drama have been unable to hear this latest contribution to a National Theatre. Let us hear the play. After all, human nature is fairly uniform, and if 'The Playboy of the Western World' is false to Irish nature, it is probably false to human nature. In that case, it is a defective play. But let us hear it.—Yours,

PADRAIC COLUM.

30 Chelmsford road
January 30, 1907[22]

Two other samples of letters to the editor should be quoted to indicate the quality of the debate which was being carried on. The play had become a cause célèbre, *and some lively discussion of art was one result:*

'THE PLAYBOY' AT THE ABBEY THEATRE

To the Editor of the 'Evening Mail':

SIR—If Mr. Synge wishes to turn the 'Sinn Fein' howlers into an applauding claque, he need only write a play portraying the Irish peasant as a flawless demi-god, using language as reticent as that of a Bishop when denouncing an editor who dares to think. It might, perhaps, be safer to leave out words altogether, and give a play in pantomime like 'L'Enfant Prodigue' (the artistes thinking carefully-pruned thoughts in Gaelic). However, if words may be used, let him tickle the ears of our national Master Bottom with a litany of praise; but, in doing so, he must, for obvious reasons, on no account 'hold up the mirror', for vanity is another of our inalienable rights.

The party with the selfish and anti-Christian name and aim of 'Sinn Fein' has not an artist within its narrow ranks, nor with the distorted outlook is it likely to produce one; but I am sure that a peasant painted to its specification would be an idyllic thing, a la Watteau, rather than a rugged actuality in the manner of say, Van Ostade.

The idyllic or Dresden type of shepherd or shepherdess has a prettiness of its own, but lovers of truth find beauty also in peasant types presented in homely surroundings, by the old Dutch masters, and by

54

painters and sculptors of our time, such as Millet, Meunier, and Rodin. Words to the author are as pigment to the painter, both are merely vehicles of expression, and if Mr. Synge's art is analogous to that of the masters named, it is, of course, too beautiful for the romantic ideals of the hyper-sensitive and cultured young men who nightly make their demonstration in a dignified manner at the Abbey Theatre to show that this is the Island of Saints.

I know some who heard and enjoyed the play on Saturday night, but altered their opinions on Monday morning in obedience to their 'Freeman's' leader. They are now the loudest of the howlers, and I know—that up to the time when they left the country to serve their apprenticeship at the linen counter in one of our big drapery houses— they never knew that a certain garment was known by any other name than the 'offending word' used by the 'Playboy'. Yours truly,

'LA LINGUE'.

31st January, 1907[23]

Letter to Irish Times:

SIR,—The battle between 'The Playboy of the Western World' and The Abbey Theatre pit is the old battle between realism and the forces of reaction, with which we are already familiar in other forms of art. When Manet, discarding convention and the 'Ideal', painted real ladies in real gardens, playing with real babies, the Paris public was scandalised—quite as scandalised as it was by 'L'Olympe', in which the same modernity, the same truth, held sway. People had been so long accustomed to regard art as a medium by which they are enabled to 'see through a glass darkly', that sunlight and reality staggered and blinded them. Parallels in music and in literature will occur to everyone. The ultimate victory, of course, remains with the artist— if he is an artist; the Philistine invariably triumphs for the moment, and usually blows many trumpets to keep up his courage.

The Freeman's Journal calls Mr. Synge's play 'a calumny on the Irish people'. But Mr. Synge has not professed to put the whole Irish race on the stage in 'The Playboy'. What he does profess to do is to present a realistic study of certain people and certain incidents. The question is not whether Mr. Synge's peasants are the only—or even the usual—types of Irish peasant character, but whether they are true to themselves and to life. I claim that they are, and that they are at least as convincing as the blameless and attenuated specimens of

55

humanity that we are so familiar with in the work of contemporary Irish writers of fiction. The banner of 'Erin and Virtue' has been worn a little threadbare of late by some of its supporters. A conspiracy of silence helps neither art nor life.

The three or four score disturbers of the Abbey Theatre performance last night gave everyone present an admirable study of the 'stage Irishman' whom they affected to disown. Mr. Synge did not need to go beyond the doors of the theatre for material for another 'calumny'. If, however, he should venture into the streets which surround that theatre, and describe in all its unlovely detail the typical life and the typical language of the Dublin slums, he would certainly produce a drama even less calculated to satisfy the idealistic aspirations of the Abbey 'pit'. We are accustomed to these sights and sounds; they are forced upon us as we walk through the city. But then, that is 'real life', from which we evidently wish to escape, and which we desire to ignore—most of all when we go to the theatre. The humanity of the proceeding I leave to the moralist, with whose mission the artist has nothing to do. But at least there is this to be said for the artist—that he is not indifferent to the spectacle of life, and that his sympathy penetrates beneath 'the shows of things'.

The question remains whether unrelieved peasant human nature is a legitimate subject for drama. If it is—and we have had little else from the modern Irish playwright—then I maintain that it should not be cribbed, cabined, and confined within certain well-defined limits, but that it should have full scope to express itself in its own language and in its own way. The old-fashioned stage peasants do very well for comic opera; they are part of the furniture of the piece; but it is quite another affair when the peasant is treated seriously as dramatic material. We do not ask what Mr. Yeats calls 'the drama of the drawing-room' to give us types; we ask it to give us real men and women. It is the same with the drama of the village.

Unless the dramatist has studied the peasant intimately and personally he is sure to bore us with banalities; or, as in the case of many of the productions of the Abbey Theatre, to give us snippets, not plays—quite charming snippets, it is true, but not to be regarded as serious drama. To a great many people, however, it will seem that it is impossible to construct really fine plays out of material so undeveloped, so little self-conscious, so limited in its range as the peasant mind. At least it is to be regretted that the contemporary Irish dramatist has not sometimes fared further afield.

With regard to 'The Playboy', considered solely as a work of art, I think it inferior to 'The Well of the Saints' and 'Riders to the Sea', not because of its realism, but because the underlying psychological idea—the stimulating effect of hero worship, following upon a life-time of suppression—is not sufficiently brought out. It is obscured by the wealth of dialogue and incidents; and the piece, at first hearing, has an air of superficiality lacking in Mr. Synge's earlier work. As to the dialogue—I am not now speaking of its decorative adjuncts— it is the most masterly study we have yet had in this *genre*.

I was surprised to see in your account of last night's performance that there had been no complaints from the audience which would have justified the expulsion of the riotous element. I was under the impression that everyone in the stalls protested audibly, and many, like myself, were astonished that no use was made by the management of the able-bodied policemen who lined the walls of the pit. It seemed an extraordinary moment to choose for a policy of non-resistance, and it was certainly hardly fair to those who wished to hear the play, and who were compelled instead to endure a two-hours' pan-demonium. Yours, etc.

ELLEN DUNCAN.

January 29th, 1907[24]

Thursday's papers also repeat the statement of the theatre's directors that the play will go on until it has been heard:

FUTURE OF THE PLAY

Lady Gregory, seen last evening, said that the directors of the Theatre intended to continue to produce 'The Playboy' until it was given a fair hearing. There was hope, she said, in the attention ac-corded it last night, and if matters improved it would come off on Saturday night as originally intended. Otherwise it would be repeated as long as necessary.

Messrs. Yeats and Synge declare that they have nothing to add to the remarks already published from them.

Mr. W. G. Fay agreed with Lady Gregory, and said that although he has no personal interest in the play beyond that of an artist, he believed it should be continued until it was made or killed by a responsible audience and not by a crowd of young men who paid their

57

money to amuse themselves and prevent the play getting a fair hearing.[25]

Looking at the Dublin riots with slight disdain, the Belfast press took an opportunity to review, damningly, the progress of the Abbey Theatre:

'PEGEEN MIKE'—A PARRICIDE—PERSONALITIES—AND PRETENCES.

Apart from the broad principles involved the situation in Dublin created by the production of Mr. J. M. Synge's 'Playboy of the Western World' has features of piquant personal interest. Mr. Synge has written a play which has been characterised as an insulting monstrosity and a vile caricature of Irish people by three-fourths of the daily Press of Dublin, and whose dirty and blasphemous language is not defended by even the 'Irish Times'. This play has been violently interrupted and fiercely hissed and hooted by Irishmen in Dublin. The police have been called in to 'quell' the tumult raised by the indignant populace. A torrent of execration has been the nightly reward of the actors who strive to represent a murderer, an idiot, some vulgar, shameless, unnatural viragoes with the soul and tongues of strumpets, and a medley of drunken mindless brutes, as typical peasants of the Gaelic County of Mayo. Let us see whence all this arose.

One Miss Horniman, an English lady, had a hall in Lower Abbey Street fitted up as a sort of 'bijou' theatre to be devoted almost exclusively to Irish drama of the higher type. We all understood that a serious effort was at last being made to banish the offensive and intolerable 'stage' Irishman and Irish woman, and to put Irish men and Irish women on the stage. The little house was handed over to literary persons who very significantly called it 'The National Theatre'. Mr. William Butler Yeats is, it seems, the Managing Director of the 'National Theatre Company'; associated with him are Lady Gregory, Mr. Edward Martyn, Mr. E. W. [sic] Fay (who acts), Mr. J. M. Synge, and, possibly, some others.

Mr. Yeats is a poet. He wrote a number of long poems, many lyrics which were not without a weird flavour of beauty, but which were never sung twice, and not one of which five persons in the country could repeat without a book, and a number of 'plays', including 'The Countess Caitlin', in which a great lady was represented as selling

58

her soul to the devil. Mr. Yeats may not believe in the existence of evil spirits: he is said to pin his faith to the actual presence of fairies on the earth, and it is certain that he wrote an 'Introduction' to one of Lady Gregory's books, in the course of which he openly advocated a return to the primitive paganism of the days when the more or less mythical Cuculain and his companions made all Ireland almost as exciting a district as the 'National Theatre' these nights. Then, Mr. Yeats had figured as an Irish Nationalist. He had temporarily left 'Art' and fairyland to harangue thousands of very material persons from a Ninety-Eight platform in the Phoenix Park now nearly nine years ago. He has identified himself, to an extent, with the Gaelic movement. He has kept himself in public notice by parading his Irishism. Mr. Yeats is, next to the author, responsible for the intro- duction to Christian civilisation in Dublin of 'Christy Mahon', the boastful parricide; 'Pegeen Mike', the shameless brute in petticoats who 'harbours' the parricide and woos him; 'Flaherty', the drunkard who goes forth to revel at a 'wake' leaving his daughter alone in a public-house under the 'protection' of the parricide; the 'Widow Quin', who strives to bring the parricide to the cabin in which she lives alone; and all the horde of bestial idiots, women and men, pic- tured as the members of this 'typical' Mayo community.

Lady Gregory is a woman of mature years, and her prominent association with this business is, on that account, very regrettable. She lives in Galway, and is, we believe, in 'comfortable' circumstances, being the widow of a late very respectable gentleman connected with the British Government in Ireland. Some years ago a very clever prose version of the Cuculain tales was published over her name— it was to this volume Mr. Yeats prefixed an introduction deifying it as 'the best book that ever came out of Ireland', and preaching paganism as an addendum to his praise. Does Lady Gregory, a Protestant—as are Mr. Yeats and Mr. Synge—know Irish Catholic girls in Galway or Mayo who would play in real life the parts of 'Pegeen Mike', the 'Widow Quin', and their female companions of 'the Western World?' Her public appearance as a champion of libellous bestiality on the Irish stage was, under all the circumstances, a sad spectacle.

Mr. Edward Martyn, of Tillyra Castle, has not as yet identified openly with 'Christy Mahon', 'Pegeen Mike' and Company. He is, we understand, a Director of this remarkable 'National Theatre, ... We expect to hear Mr. Martyn's opinion of Mr. Yeats, Lady Gregory,

Mr. Synge, 'Christy Mahon', 'Pegeen Mike', and drunken 'Flaherty' very soon. He cannot well remain silent. The young men who are vigorously protesting against the nightly outrages at Lower Abbey, Dublin, include several believers in the 'policy' of the 'National Council' presided over by Mr. Martyn of the 'National Theatre' and the Kildare Street Club. Ireland surely is—in some details—a 'Land of Contradictions'.

Tuesday night found another addition to the 'National Theatre' troupe: no less a person than Mr. P. D. Kenny, *alias* 'Pat'. This eminent 'economist' began his 'public career' in Ireland as a 'Special Correspondent' in Connaught for the 'Irish Times' at a period when all the resources of calumny were allied to all the rascalities of Coercion against the growth of the United Irish League. He figured afterwards as the editor of the 'Irish Peasant', and it was only a week or two ago he published somewhere a glowing account of his trials and vicissitudes, exploits and triumphs, in connection with that ill-fated organ. Mr. Kenny also published a volume of fragmentary essays, mainly devoted to puerile self-laudation, and occasionally diverging into attacks on the Irish priesthood which won the hearts of those who had previously taken Mr. Michael F. J. M'Carthy to their bosoms. On Tuesday night Mr. 'Pat' Kenny appeared at the 'National Theatre' and howled appeals from the stalls on behalf of 'Christy Mahon' and 'Pegeen Mike' —playing an excellent 'second fiddle' to the drunken Galwegian and the yelping pack from Trinity College who foregathered to applaud Mr. Synge and Lady Gregory, Mr. Yeats, and 'Pegeen'.

Yesterday's 'Irish Times'—the journal of his early anti-United Irish League efforts—had an article from the pen of this strange and wonderful 'Irish Irelander' (!) Mr. P. D. Kenny, vehemently insisting upon the strict truth to life in Mayo of the 'highly moral play'. He wrote of 'the merciless accuracy of his (Mr. Synge's) revelation', praised his 'moral courage', made a most elaborate analysis of the dramatist's 'motives', which, of course, were of the highest and noblest kind, and were set forth in the most delightful, convincing, and 'subtle' manner.

Unhappily, yesterday's papers also contained an interview with Mr. Synge, stating that he had no grand, deep, 'subtle', ulterior motives—that his play was simply an 'extravaganza' founded on the story of 'Lynchehaun's' escape and some incident in the Aran Islands.

60

'Pat' should have consulted the author before weaving his 'economics' of high 'morality' around the wretched, dunderheaded farrago of blasphemy, obscenity, and caricature. 'Sermons in stones' is a fanciful idea enough. . . .

Having dealt with the personalities directly responsible for this unpleasant and unsavoury episode, we leave them to Irish Irelanders who are, like the members of our own Ulster Little Theatre, pure of mind and heart and truly Irish in their instincts. There are a few other considerations worth noting.

All this cant and rant about 'Art' by Yeats and Synge is the veriest humbug—old, exploded, meaningless humbug, too. These men call their playhouse 'The National Theatre'. Let them shed the misnomer, remove the words 'National' and 'Irish' from their theatre, their programmes, their plays, and all their proceedings and belongings, and we, of Ireland and for Ireland, will have no further right to complain. 'Pat', Lady Gregory, the 'God-Save-King' students of Trinity, who 'cheered lustily for the parricide', according to yesterday's 'News-Letter'—the drunken squireen from Galway, who bawled and hiccoughed and screamed, and 'd---d' after the fashion of Mr. Synge's 'peasants', and offered to fight everyone in vindication of 'Art', 'morality', and 'truth'—these, and those who think with them, will be then quite at liberty to patronise the Yeats-Synge plays, and applaud parricides and 'Pegeen Mikes' to the content of their elevated and artistic hearts. But let the farce of representing this foul rubbish as 'National' or 'Irish' drama be dropped in common decency.

If the exploiters of 'Christy Mahon' and 'Pegeen Mike' chose to present 'realistic' sketches of the language and manners of a Parisian den of infamy and to locate the den in Galway or County Down, would their work be accepted as a 'subtle' moral sermon? Or would papers published in Ireland appeal on its behalf as a needed though 'dreadful searchlight into our cherished accumulation of social skeletons?' One can imagine no abomination that could not be defended by the pleas put forward on behalf of 'The Playboy of the Western World'. But the public are the jury, and their verdict must be accepted. If this verdict is not heeded or meeded by the Yeats-Synge gentry, let them carefully guard their doors, drop the false pretences implied in the words 'National' and 'Irish', and avoid all danger of opposition or censure by relying for support and criticism on 'Pat', the intoxicated man from Galway, the God-save-the-King boys of Trinity who admire parricides, and the 'Irish Times', which loves 'remorseless truth' so well that it discovers the precious thing in the abominations woven round 'Christy Mahon' and 'Pegeen Mike'.[26]

By Thursday night the disturbances had begun to decrease:

ABBEY THEATRE PLAY

A FAIR HEARING ACCORDED

The fifth performance of Mr. Synge's new comedy, 'The Playboy of the Western World' took place last evening at the Abbey Theatre. Again there was a large and mixed audience, again there was a strong body of police stationed inside and outside the building, and again boohing, hissing, stamping, and applauding occurred throughout the course of the play; but, for the first time, the piece was accorded a fair hearing, and no disorder of a serious nature took place. When the curtain rose on the preceding play, 'Riders to the Sea', almost all the seats in the pit were occupied, and there was a good attendance in the gallery; but there were many empty seats in the stalls. The walls on either side of the pit were lined with stalwart constables and officers in plain clothes and in uniform were judiciously scattered about in all parts of the building ready for any emergency. Outside the theatre there appeared to be the same number of constables on duty as on the previous evening. The opening play was listened to with great attention, and all the good points were loudly applauded.

When the play which has aroused so much criticism commenced there was a chorus of hissing and boohing, intermingled with outbursts of applause, but these expressions of feeling soon subsided, and for a while the first act proceeded with very few punctuations of this character. Later some more boohing and hissing occurred, but the words spoken on the stage were never drowned for any length of time, and some portions of the act were enthusiastically received even in the pit. There were certainly more interruptions in the second act, in which the major portion of the contentious matter is introduced, but there was no real disturbance, as on the previous evening. The word 'shift', which comes in here, was again howled at for a few seconds. Good humour was restored when the expression 'Jim would get drunk on the smell of a pint' was made use of, and someone in the pit called out, 'That's not Western life'. At the close of this act a burly young fellow in the front of the pit started to sing in lusty tones, 'The men of the West', and the chorus was taken up by those around him. The solo went on with a fair amount of success, until the orchestra struck up an Irish air. The 'broken melody', however, did no harm, and the third act opened very quietly. It had not proceeded very far when for no particular reason apparently about a dozen young men in the pit rose and left the building, booing and hissing as they went.

Between the first and third acts, however, the gathering in the pit had been considerably augmented, and the vacant seats were soon filled. Several present, in fact, could not find seating accommodation, and had to stand alongside 'men in blue'. Booing, stamping and applause occurred alternately throughout the remaining portion of the play, but it was of a more or less subdued character. Although one man in the pit became so disorderly that he had to be forcibly removed by the police, on the whole the piece received, as we have said, a fair hearing, and the audience left the building in good order.[27].

Although some attributed the changed atmosphere within the theatre to revisions in the text, Lady Gregory denied that much had been bowdlerized. All three directors of the theatre issued statements of their satisfaction at the diminishing of protests during the play:

A WEEDING-OUT OF WORDS

Lady Gregory, seen at the conclusion of the performance, expressed her pleasure at the hearing accorded to the play 'If Friday and Saturday nights' performances are equally satisfactory, 'The Playboy' season will end this week; if not, it will be continued until the management consider that everyone wishing to hear it has had a fair opportunity of having his wish fulfilled.

Has not the play been considerably pruned, and have not some of the expressions to which the greatest objection was made been deleted?

'Very little change has been made', said Lady Gregory. 'It is true that a few adjectives have been taken out, as have been most of the invocations of the Holy Name, but curiously enough the words and phrases to which most objection has been raised have not been interfered with'.

Lady Gregory added that a suggestion had been made that if the prices of admission were raised the disorder would have ceased at once. But they had too much confidence in the good sense of the general public to adopt that course, and she considered that the comparative tranquility that night justified their confidence.

She continued that she had been offered considerable support from the 'classes'—what some people, she said, would call the 'Castle dinner' set—if such plays as 'Kathleen ni Houlihan' were not staged. But she had declined. Another section would object to some other play, and so on until the management would be reduced to musical comedy without the comedy—simply the music.[28]

MR. SYNGE 'BEAMING'.

AUTHOR AND 'JAW-BREAKERS'.

The author, Mr. J. M. Synge, was beaming at the reception accorded to 'The Playboy' when he was approached by a representative of the 'Independent'. Beyond expressing his gratification at having at last got something like a fair hearing, he had little to say.

Our representative asked him if he thought the use of such 'jaw-breakers' as 'potentate', 'retribution', etc. were typical of the conversation of such places as that he had selected for his scene.

Mr. Synge laughingly replied that that was just the very place to hear them. He knew peasants such as he had tried to depict, taking the keenest delight in airing any big words of which they had got hold. As an instance, he said, he heard a poor old woman who was absolutely illiterate say 'I have to use all sorts of stratagems to keep the hens out'.[29]

THE POET IS PLEASED.

INTERVIEW WITH MR. YEATS.

Interviewed after the performance, Mr. Yeats expressed himself pleased with the progress of events. 'Gradually', he said, 'the audience are beginning to see what the play means. We always had the stalls with us, but to-night for the first time we had the majority of the pit on our side, and any protests that there were were perfectly fair. If members of the audience object to certain parts of the play, of course they have a perfect right to express their dissent in a reasonable way'.

They had to face the same opposition, he said, when 'The Shadow of the Glen' was first produced. The opening performance was hissed, and the hissing at the second performance was still more violent. But now it was played to most appreciative audiences, and had two curtains the other day.

Mr. Yeats pointed out that the word which describes a necessary article of female attire and which, he said, had caused all the row, appeared in Longfellow, and was a word commonly used in the West of Ireland. No peasant hesitated for a moment about using it. 'It is a good old English word', he declared.

Further referring to the hostile demonstrations that had taken place, Mr. Yeats said that events were taking the normal course of the work of a man who had a curious, a very new and harsh kind of imagination. There had been a great deal of unreal sentimentalising and idealising of the Irish peasant, and possibly there was now taking place a reaction in the other direction in Irish types of character. That was the way of literature. Ibsen's 'League of Youth' created a most frightful uproar when first produced, but eventually it became the most popular of all the Norwegian's plays.

As regards the coming production of Geroge Bernard Shaw's 'John Bull's Other Island', in Dublin, he did not think it would give rise to the same display of feeling. 'Shaw's play is merely a debate', he said, 'and he gives both sides'.

If the play continues during the week to receive the same support that it did last night, Mr. Yeats said, they will have achieved their object, and will not continue it next week. In any event, it will be produced on Monday. That evening will be devoted to a discussion of the play, in which any member of the public may take part.[30]

Again on Friday night there was practically no disorder in the theatre and the performance went smoothly, although the police were still present inside and outside the theatre. After the performance there was a brief and peaceful demonstration in Marlborough Street, opposite the theatre, in which Mr. Wall, the magistrate who had criticized the production, was cheered.

Now, the weekly journals began their onslaught of the play. In its edition dated 2 February, Sinn Fein, *edited by Arthur Griffith, features this editorial:*

The Abbey Theatre: The management of the Abbey Theatre has sent us the following advertisement to occupy a column of our space:

SUPPORT ABBEY THEATRE

AGAINST

ORGANISED OPPOSITION

HE WHO STRIKES AT

FREEDOM OF JUDGMENT

STRIKES

AT THE SOUL OF THE NATION.

NEW PLAY

EVERY EVENING

TILL FURTHER NOTICE.

We visited the Abbey Theatre on Tuesday night to exercise our freedom of judgment, and as a result we decline to print as an advertisement what the Abbey Theatre management has forwarded us. The opposition is not 'organised'—it is the opposition of the public. However, we print it free of charge as the defence of the Abbey Theatre management for what is taking place on the stage each night.

Mr. Synge's play as a play is one of the worst constructed we have witnessed. As a presentation on the public stage it is a vile and inhuman story told in the foulest language we have ever listened to from a public platform. The play represents the peasant women of Mayo contending in their lusts for the possession of a man who has appealed to their depraved instincts by murdering, as they believe, his father. Later, they discover the supposed parricide to be an imposter, and in rage drive him forth. This hideous story is told in language much of which is too coarse to be printed in any public journal. The author declares that the words and phrases he used he has himself heard spoken. We have no doubt of it. We heard no phrase on the stage of the Abbey Theatre which may not be heard on the lips of the dregs of humanity, but we have yet to learn that it is realism or art to reproduce on a public stage the language of the gutter.

The father of the hero refers to his son in one place as 'a dirty —————— lout'. The word omitted is so obscene that no man of ordinary decency would use it, and certainly no man, unless an utterly degraded one, would use it in the presence of a woman. In the Abbey Theatre it is represented as being used in conversation between a Mayo peasant man and a Mayo peasant woman. We observed a man who hissed this vile expression being roughly seized by two policemen and thrust out of the theatre.

The author of the play presents it as true to Irish life. He declares in the programme that 'the central incident of the Playboy'—that is the fighting of the women of the West for the hand of a parricide because he is a parricide—'was suggested by an actual occurrence in the West'. This is a definite statement, and if the author can sustain it, we shall regret that so vile a race should be permitted to exist. If, on the other hand, the author's statement is untrue—his play can only be considered as the production of a moral degenerate.

On Tuesday this story of unnatural murder and unnatural lust, told in foul language was told under the protection of a body of police, and concluded to the strains of 'God Save the King'. The circumstances were appropriate, but we are sorry for the Abbey Theatre. It invited the opinion of the public upon its play, and when that opinion was unfavourable it invited the aid of Dublin Castle to crush its expression. And yet its directors talk of 'freedom'. We have never yet understood by that word in connection with the Press licence to publish obscenity or licence to libel with impunity. In connection with the drama it is evidently the definition of the directors of the Abbey Theatre, who seem to have now got hopelessly away from life. With the aid of the police and 'God Save the King' much may be accomplished in Ireland, but even such potent influences will not be strong enough to make the Irish people cry 'Ecco lo fico!' to Mr. J. M. Synge.[31]

Ambrose Power was quick to correct the accusation that he had spoken obscene language:

DEAR SIR—My attention has been drawn to the following passage in your issue of to-day:—'The father of the hero refers to his son in one place as "a dirty —————— lout'. The word omitted is so obscene that no man of ordinary decency would use it, and certainly no man, unless an utterly degraded one, would use it in the presence of a woman'.

I am the actor referred to as having spoken the word you mention. The word which you indicate by a dash was in the text, and as I spoke it on the stage 'stuttering'. I fail to see anything obscene in the word.

I demand an immediate and public withdrawal and apology.—
Yours faithfully,

AMBROSE POWER.[32]

And Arthur Griffith retracted his accusation.

But Sinn Fein's *attack was mild when compared with that which the* Freeman's Journal *had been carrying on, or the comments appearing in* The Leader *of that Saturday:*

We think the Abbey Theatre people made a great blunder in staging the play at all. Having staged it, and announced it to run for seven nights, they show that they are only human after all in not feeling inclined to retire before the hostile reception it has met with. However, they would have been well advised had they withdrawn the piece in consequence of the reception accorded its first performance by the audience and the Press. A mistake was made in bringing in the police, but after a while the police were ordered off by the authorities of the theatre. There were two wills at play on Monday night, which could not have been brought into collision without results that would probably be most deplorable. As it was, both wills had their way without a collision. The opposition to the play refused it a hearing, and gained its object, and the players played right through the play, and so carried out their programme. Apart from one's feelings or views in relation to the play, it was impossible not to admire the pluck of the actors and actresses in a situation that called for all their reserve of nerve. The opposition was large and resolute, and had the police been ordered to interfere, we doubt if some of the protestors would have been willing to leave the theatre without a struggle that, from every point of view, would have been regrettable.

Passions are inflamed now, and the Abbey Theatre people, we see, have decided to fight the matter out. The manifesto they have issued may indicate pluck, but we do not think it is wise. . . .

The authorities of the theatre endeavour to elevate the squabble into one of Organised Opposition *versus* Freedom of Judgment. Might

we point out that though some of the opposition may have been organised, the spontaneous and independent opposition is very great
and very strong, and that 'freedom of judgment' sounds all right as a
phrase, but will not necessarily convince people who regard it as a
misnomer for freedom of slander, and for freedom for hurling obscene insults at the peasants of Mayo; indeed, as the peasantry of
Ireland are a class in themselves—and the biggest class in Ireland—
the 'freedom of judgment' indulged in by Mr. Synge is a matter that
concerns all the mere Irish. Mr. Synge has apparently outraged Irish
feeling, and the authorities of the theatre are, we think, ill-advised
in fighting the cause of what they call 'freedom of judgment' with such
a weapon as 'The Playboy of the Western World'.[33]

'THE PLAYBOYS IN THE ABBEY'

The unmistakable, vigorous and spontaneous outburst of disapproval which practically put an end to the last act of Mr. Synge's
gruesome farce at the Abbey Theatre last Saturday can only be regretted on the score that it was so long delayed. Visitors to the Abbey
Theatre are now familiarised with the conception of Irish character
held by the coterie of playwriters whose works are staged there, but
they were scarcely prepared for the ghastly freak of fancy to which
they were treated under the guise of a comedy, entitled 'The
Playboy of the Western World'. It may be too much to hope that the
protest will have substantial effect on a theatre not depending on
public support, but it is at least some satisfaction that that protest has
been made.

Mr. Synge calls his play a comedy, and the essential humour of the
piece lies in the fact that the 'hero', who becomes the idol of the
peasants because he has murdered his father, is really not entitled to
this worship since he has merely attempted the crime. This side-
splitting jest constitutes the 'plot' of the play. Sane people who have
not seen the piece will scarcely credit this; it seems too awful, too
grotesque. But then this play is the Triumph of the Grotesque, or, at
least, it was to have been if the audience had not thought differently.
The grotesque may be defensible; it may have its attractions for certain
morbid minds; but much depends on the subject that is dealt with
through this medium, and when filial affection, the sacredness of life,
and the modesty of women are selected for this treatment, simple

69

persons not endowed with the true artistic temperament may be pardoned if they decline to approve.

The absolute eccentricity of the central idea of the play seemed at first to place it beyond the region of ordinary criticism, and to this fact must, no doubt, in large measure be attributed the tolerance and good humour with which the first and second acts were received; yet this is but a poor excuse to offer in extenuation of the measure of favour accorded to the piece. It is no exaggeration to say that had the production been submitted to the less artistic appreciation of a commercial audience, it would have been hooted off the stage in half an hour. Of course, the author and the clique who are associated with what has been felicitously described as the Movement in the Morgue, take pride to themselves that this is so. They claim that their works are unsuited for the common air; they are precious plants, and need the neurotic atmosphere of the Abbey in which to thrive.

Objection to 'The Playboy of the Western World' is based on more grounds than one. We Irish are sometimes charged with being too sensitive, with disliking to see our faults portrayed in play or story. That charge may be true enough, yet it is perhaps not unreasonable that we should consider our case unfairly stated when nothing but our faults were shown. It is to this that the agitation against the 'Stage Irishman' owes its origin. Now the characters—male and female—in Mr. Synge's play are devoid of any redeeming quality whatever. In a speech some two years ago on the plays of Mr. Synge, Mr. Yeats said, speaking of the Irish people—'We are no moral monsters'. The characters in 'The Playboy' are immoral monstrosities. A broken-down, evil-looking tramp enters a low public-house on the coast of Mayo, and after some inquiry admits to those gathered there that he has murdered his father. The doubting, mistrustful attitude of his hearers at once changes into one of awe and admiration. He is installed as pot-boy at the request of the publican's daughter, and is left in charge of the shebeen by the father.

In the second act we are shown the countryside flocking to pay homage to the man who, in the language of the dramatist, has 'killed his da'. The women are depicted wooing with no trace of modesty this delightful type of strong, passionate man. Pegeen-Mike, the publican's daughter, jilts her timid betrothed for him. Ultimately, however, the supposed murdered parent turns up, and recognises his son, whose popularity then declines as a natural consequence.

This extravagant and fantastic conceit is spun out into three acts.

70

It is not improbable that the patience of the audience would have been exhausted by the wearisome vulgarity and laboured buffoonery of the third act, even had their wrath not been aroused by the wanton indecency of a particular passage of the dialogue. As it was, a certain sentence, which has possibly been since omitted, served to provoke a disturbance that would have been as welcome as it was deserved much earlier in the evening. It is scarcely conceivable that Mr. Synge will seriously argue that parricide is regarded in Ireland as one of the virtues, as his comedy would have us believe. More probable is it that he will inform us that the eye of the artist sees no petty distinctions of nationality, that his characters are types to be met with throughout the world, given names and local habitations simply for convenience. With this style of argument we are becoming familiar, but we may safely reply that Mr. Synge's types are not merely un-Irish, they are inhuman.

Possibly, looking at the matter from this point, Mr. Synge is merely a writer of comedies endowed with a somewhat peculiar conception of humour. What is however, most striking about his latest playful effort is the extraordinary decadence of tone which pervades it from start to finish. What is most surprising about the audience on the first night was their apparent inability to realise this till the performance was almost ended. Throughout the play there runs an undercurrent of animalism and irreligion really as rare in the much-decried Theatre of Commerce as it is undesirable in what purports to be the National Theatre of Ireland. One looks in vain for a glimmer of Christianity in the acts or utterances of the characters. Superadded must be the frequent repetition of words for the use of what any corner-boy would be arrested, and touches of coarse buffoonery, which would not be tolerated in a pantomime.

Such was 'The Playboy of the Western World' as performed on Saturday last. Should such plays continue to be the class of entertainment given in the National Theatre, criticism must eventually take the form of cabbage. AVIS.[34]

Although the directorate was winning its fight by persevering in presenting the play, its action caused one damaging defection: William Boyle, who had been the most popular of the Abbey's playwrights, the one on whom they had relied for certain box office success, wrote:

To the Editor of the *Freeman's Journal:*

71

SIR,—As the writer of plays recently produced at the Abbey Theatre, I beg to say that I have written to Mr. Yeats to-day withdrawing from his company my sanction to the performances of any play of mine in the future. This is my protest against the present attempt to set up a standard of National Drama based on the vilification of any section of the Irish People, in a theatre ostensibly founded for the production of plays to represent real Irish life and character.—I am etc.

WILLIAM BOYLE.[35]

Boyle's withdrawal, effected before he had even read the play, evoked this reply from the critic, Stephen Gwynn:

To the Editor of the *Freeman's Journal*:

DEAR SIR,—It is the simplest thing in life, and the cheapest, to kill a play. All the public has to do is to stay away from the theatre. If you go to fight it, the conflict develops whatever is strong in the piece; and so much as this is clear about Mr. Synge's work—it possesses notably the quality of strength, especially when acted by Mr. Fay's Company. But he has undoubtedly put his admirers into a very difficult position, and, for my own part, I do not in the least regret that the play was hissed at its first performance, for the very good reason that if it were played with acceptance, word would immediately go out that parricide is a popular exploit in Ireland. The mass of mankind who do not look closely into distinctions would have jumped to the conclusion I indicate, all the more readily because Mr. Synge has taken an unfair advantage of certain notorious facts.

It is notorious, to begin with, that among the Irish peasantry there is every disposition to shelter a man who is wanted by the police. By a very old tradition, based on the general injustice of the mode of government, Irish peasants are banded together against the criminal law. Hence, for instance, the escape of Lynchehaun. Mr. Synge would go on to argue, I fancy, that from this traditional attitude there springs among very primitive peasants a moral result in an absence of reprobation for crimes of violence. The sheltered murderer, he would say, is rather an object of curiosity than of horror. Many of us would dissent vehemently from that deduction, except in cases when the killing is regarded as an act of civil war. But, if the deduction be conceded, it is easy to see how grim imagination can shape out a lonely inert community where nothing happens, in which the man who has

72

done a deed is a man of note—and, by another step forward along the same consistent line of exaggeration, the more notable in proportion to the horror of his deed. The result is a distortion of life, literally speaking untrue, yet in a true relation to life. The fourth book of 'Gulliver' is not true literally, and it is not at all pretty; but it is artistically defensible. Artistically I have not a word to say against Mr. Synge, for the facts out of which his exaggeration springs exist unquestionably, and no good critic will take his play as a social document, a literal impeachment, of Irish country people. But practically I recognise that if the play succeeded it would be held as justifying the view which represents Ireland as peopled by a murderous race of savages.

For that reason, when Mr. Synge invents a community without any natural repugnance to the idea of homicide, and brings into it a young man much oppressed by fear and by conscience after killing his father, in order to show the comic effect of surroundings upon character, it seems to me our best course is to say that we know very well Mr. Synge is joking, but that we do not like his turn of humour. It is neither wise nor fair, I say (with all respect to the Freeman and other authorities) to assert that he is deliberately vilifying the Irish people; and I regret particularly that Mr. Boyle should have joined in the cry. He is laying down the law to his own hurt, for the thing has been made into a contest of lungs against brains; and to-morrow an audience may discover that the 'Building Fund' does not represent Ireland to their liking. For my own part, I would say that if I took the plays as documents, none have presented Irishmen and Irishwomen in so unattractive a light as Mr. Boyle's. The central springs of action in his pieces are mean motives; more especially, the family group in the 'Building Fund' is as repulsive as anything could be. It is mordant satire and legitimate satire; but it would give to any outside judge the impression that the Irish were a detestable people far more, surely, than any work of Mr. Synge's. A man of letters himself, Mr. Boyle would, I am sure, never form from a sight or reading of the play the conclusion on which he so precipitately severs his connection with the theatre—that Mr. Synge is deliberately vilifying his countrymen. Or would Mr. Boyle, I wonder, feel called upon to stand up and hiss when Pegeen Mike retorts to the Widow Quin's protest that she has come in merely to buy a penn'orth of starch—'You that had never shirt nor shift in the house with you'. Does anyone really assert—anyone who knows peasants in any country—that a scolding vixen

73

of a peasant girl would never bring her tongue to say 'shift?' My experience of Irish peasant people is that they have all the real natural delicacy, and none of the artificial. Generally speaking, they will use freely any word which would consort with the language of poetry, and 'shift' is such a word. It is only when you come to washerwomen's elegant equivalents that delicacy begins. I take this merely as an instance of the way in which mob clamour against a work of art will tend to set every man who cares for art on the side of the artist; and I am sorry that Mr. Boyle, an artist himself, should step out of the rank and hand himself with those who wish to deny another writer his natural privilege, which is to say his say to those who choose to hear him. No man and no woman is forced to hear or to read.—Yours faithfully,

STEPHEN GWYNN.[36]

Boyle, in his answer, appeals to 'The audience is always right' theory, and sees the protest as a kind of justified censorship:

To the Editor of the *Freeman's Journal:*

DEAR SIR,—Mr. Stephen Gwynn states that he regrets particularly that I should have joined in the cry of the people against 'The Playboy of the Western World', which he characterises as a contest of lungs against brains. He adds that I am laying down a law to my own hurt, for to-morrow an audience may find that 'The Building Fund' does not represent Ireland to their liking, and proceeds to give them a lead by saying that, for his part, no plays have presented Irishmen and Irishwomen in so unattractive a light as mine have. One of the reasons which determined me to make my protest against Mr. Synge's play on the reports of it in the newspapers was the fact that the Irish public has accepted my criticisms of certain phases of Irish character, although they are, of course, satirical, and, therefore, of course, unflattering. The very fact that this same public had accepted my satire good-naturedly convinced me that they were not protesting without good cause against 'The Playboy of the Western World'. If they had denounced my plays I should not have allowed the management of the National Theatre to continue to force the presentment of them; nor should I have appealed to party spirit to sustain my art with the aid of police, at the risk of a riot.

This question is a larger one than the Abbey Theatre directors appear to realise. In England there is a censor, who reads all plays, and cuts out offensive words and passages; or, if the play be generally offensive, refuses to license its performance. This censorship is objected to by some, of whom the most notable is the distinguished critic, Mr. William Archer. Writing in 'The Tribune', a week ago, Mr. Archer said—'The censor satisfies no one, except the managers who want to produce "risky" plays, and if his office were abolished, the true censor—the decent-minded public—would awake to its duty, and they (the managers) could not vend their wares with anything like the security they now enjoy'. Because there is no censor in Ireland this 'decent-minded public' proceeding to do what Mr. Archer calls 'its duty', results in several people being denounced to the police and fined by a reluctant magistrate. Mr. Gwynn suggests the public could express disapproval 'by staying away'. It is curious that when they stayed away from some of Mr. Synge's former plays these plays still went on, because the 'Abbey' is a subsidised theatre, independent of the money taken at the door. Therefore, realising that the public had no remedy, but the one resorted to, I made the protest to which Mr. Gwynn takes exception.—Yours, etc.,

WILLIAM BOYLE.[37]

Gwynn's letter also provoked other letters appearing in Monday's papers, all from people prominent in Irish literary circles. D. J. O'Donoghue, the well-respected editor and biographer of Carleton, Mangan, and others, writes:

DEAR SIR,—I so rarely intervene in a newspaper controversy that perhaps you will allow me to press my surprise that a writer of much acumen as Mr. Stephen Gwynn should allow his dislike of 'The Building Fund'—a dislike quite well known to readers of the Freeman—to tempt him into the queer comparison between Mr. Boyle's play and 'The Playboy'. I cannot see the remotest analogy. Mr. Boyle represents his chief character as a miser, with all the callousness and harshness of a miser, and without the slightest feeling of affection for his cranky and miserly mother. Surely this is a consistent piece of character-drawing? Shawn Grogan is a hateful character, no doubt, mean and sordid, but Boyle does not make him a hero. Nobody in the play worships him, or makes amorous advances to him, or applauds his courage—and he must have had a considerable amount of it—and all his dodgery and meanness end in defeat. Where is the analogy between 'The Building Fund' and 'The Playboy'?

75

Shawn Grogan is detestable—nearly as detestable as Christopher Mahon—but the irresistible humour of Boyle makes one forget the miser's lack of filial affection and his sordidness. The result is doubtless unedifying, but I do not deplore the humour of the author. It enabled him to give Mr. Fay a chance of which that admirable comedian made the most.

I do not see how 'The Playboy' gains by Mr. Gwynn's comparison. As presented at first, I regarded it as a seriously meant contribution to the drama. It now appears as an extravaganza, and is played as such. And yet it lacks the essentials of an extravaganza. The continuous ferocity of the language; the consistent shamelessness of all the characters (without exception), and the persistent allusions to sacred things make the play even more inexcusable as an extravaganza than as a serious play. I prefer to regard it in the latter sense, in justice to Mr. Synge's undoubted power as a writer. As a serious play, it offends many people; as an extravaganza, it is made peculiarly vile by the many serious allusions to things which Catholic and Protestant hold sacred. To my mind, the episode of the blessing by the drunken publican is painfully gratuitous. As for the use of certain words, such as 'shift', I quite agree with Mr. Gwynn. It is simply old-maidish to affect horror when such expressions are used.

No one who knows Mr. Synge will for a moment charge him with deliberate vilification of the Irish peasantry. But there is only one other alternative. If he knows Irish peasant life as thoroughly as Mr. Yeats and others assert, then I see no other solution than that the offence is deliberate. I prefer the alternative. I am afraid Mr. Synge's play is due to ignorance of Irish life. Mr. Boyle has rashly assumed that Mr. Synge does really know the Irish peasant. Hence, I imagine, his strong and immediate expression of opinion. With his own intense sympathy for the Irish peasant, and his absolutely unrivalled knowledge of Irish town and country life, Boyle has already given us such masterpieces as 'The Eloquent Dempsy' and 'The Mineral Workers', and he ought now to give the Irish stage the finest portrayal of Irish character we have yet had. Indeed, I believe his are already the best Irish plays we possess.

May I be permitted to add a word or two as to the absurd talk of 'freedom of thought' and 'freedom of discussion'. I have no sympathy with the person who goes to the Abbey Theatre, and who, immediately the curtain rises, proceeds to stamp the floor, and in other ways tries to drown the voices of the players. I do not see that he has any grievance if he is summarily ejected and even prosecuted. But the vindictiveness which has been shown night after night in expelling and prosecuting people who, in their excitement, have called out 'It's a libel', or 'shame', or otherwise mildly protested, is a serious menace to the freedom of an audience, and that freedom is rather more important than the freedom of any playwright. Such stifling of freedom as has been witnessed in the Abbey Theatre during the past week will speedily make the theatre, and the movement it was founded to promote, stink (the word will be familiar to visitors to the Abbey) in the nostrils of the public. Moreover, I consider organised support just as disgraceful as organised opposition—more disgraceful, in truth. I am glad Mr. Synge's play—that is, the later Bowdlerised version—was given a fair hearing, as fair a hearing as the original version received on the first night. It was not (so far as I have been able to judge) until the organised support was introduced that the opposition became intensified.

Finally, have we not had enough of the cult of the tramp and beggar, especially the dirty and disreputable tramp and beggar? Only the consummate acting of the wonderful band of players in the Abbey Theatre has made some of its plays tolerable. Even their exceeding cleverness cannot make 'The Playboy' acceptable, and it may be said that they never played better—perhaps owing to the electricity of the atmosphere.

Following Mr. Gwynn's excellent example, I give my name.—Yours truly,

D. J. O'DONOGHUE.[38]

Alice Milligan, whose play The Last Feast of the Fianna *was one of the first presented by the Irish Literary Theatre, added her comments, again based on published reports only:*

To the Editor of the *Freeman's Journal:*

SIR,—I have not seen nor read the much-abused play at the Abbey Theatre, and, on general principle, I would be inclined to agree exactly with Mr. Stephen Gwynn's opinion as to the methods of opposition which were so unfortunately displayed. But, having been in a way behind the scenes in connection with the literary theatre movement in Ireland from the outset, I am aware of influences and motives that are at work, and which, now that they begin to be displayed boldly and openly, require to be met by even more effective and decisive methods. To begin with, let me say that I have never missed a performance at the Abbey Theatre when it was within my power to attend, even by undertaking a long journey from Belfast, or some country place, for the purpose. And though given to frequenting the cheap seats in other theatres, and travelling third-class on railways, I always made it a rule to take stall tickets at the Abbey for myself and some friends to accompany. I have bought all their playbooks and publications, and have been accustomed to send them to literary friends through the country, and have deprecated as far as in my power, both by voice and pen, opposition and hostility in as far as it seemed to me inspired by personal and political motives; and there is no doubt that both Mr. Yeats and the Messrs. Fay brought with them to the Abbey Theatre enterprise a considerable heritage of opposition and enmity, which they had earned in a previous stage of their joint theatrical career. It has cost me a certain amount of self-repression and self-restraint not to have been in the thick of this opposition, but as I do not reside in Dublin I need not boast of having overcome temptation. Removed from the area of strife, I have been obliged in all justice to acknowledge that the productions at the Abbey have been uniformly admirable, and from a literary point of view far ahead of anything attempted by rival societies. I would not even take exception to the much-discussed 'Shadow in (sic) the Glen', having been accustomed during my stay in Donegal last summer to hear a Gaelic ballad with the same plot much applauded by the country people and scholars. I do not draw the line at the play being morbid, or showing up the mean and sordid and reprehensible side of human character. In literature I am now inclined to prefer realism to romance. If Mr. Synge or Mr. W. Boyle could write a strong and stinging satire showing up the type of woman so common in Ireland, or, at any rate, in the Irish law courts, who sues for reparation for breach of promise of marriage, I think they would be doing a service to society, and no one would have occasion to raise a clamour against a libel on Irish womanhood. The Gaelic actors have been busy at it satirising the shoneen and professional politician, so they cannot object to satire in general.

What I object to, and what I desire to have restrained, is not realism, nor yet satire on Irish life, but simply the managing director's newfound art of advertising. In spite of the Abbey's services to Art, it has not received due support from the public, and it would seem that

78

Mr. Yeats has said to himself, and said to his playwrights, 'This will never do; we must fill the house at all costs. Let us be audacious; let us shock the public conscience and the public ideas of decency. Look at Bernard Shaw. He is a genius and a great dramatist; but he was never really recognised as such till his plays were forbidden by the Censor'.

Mr. Yeats began it himself in 'Deirdre'. Of this no more need be said than that, as the most brazened playgoers and play actors require acting expurgated editions of Shakespeare, acting expurgated editions of Yeats will be called for. But that sort of thing only frightened away and thinned an audience. With 'The Playboy' he has achieved his aim, and the crowd that hitherto stayed away filled the Abbey at last to shriek down this extravaganza of an advertisement. No wonder the managing director is delighted. If his party go over to England crowds will rush to see what it is all about.

But then—was not the theatre founded for the elevation of National drama, and for the sake of all that was intended and much that was done, cannot it be saved? Is not Lady Gregory herself a delightful humourist, literally in the position of reader to the company? We look to her to exercise due control, and not to permit the managing director's advertising tendencies to spoil the high standard of art which up till almost recently has been unmarred.

The plot of the play, as far as I can make out, is similar to that of a squalid story that I glanced at in a comic illustrated annual the day before yesterday. English magazine literature is now greatly concerned with the criminal and his surroundings. This tale, 'The Hero of Hamilton street', by a man called Pettridge, described the exit of a convict from quod, his reception by an admiring public, who made a hero of him till they discovered that the four years he had done had broken his spirit, and that he intended to give up the old business. His glory departed. He was a hero no more. Can the author of 'Riders to the Sea' give us no better than that? I hope he will yet live down his present unpopularity, caused merely by his consenting to act as sandwich man for the managing director.

As for the best means to meet with another production of this kind, I would suggest to the newspaper critics of the first night to include in their notices of the play a plain exposition of the improprieties of the play, with quotations as far as they can decently go, and then add a list of the principal people present, with a description of what the ladies wore, in the style of the fashionable intelligence.

79

If this were done in the case of some of the musical comedy abominations which come around, the audiences would be thinned of that
section of the community who go through curiosity, but would not
wish to have their presence observed. In the case of the Abbey Theatre,
at another juncture like the present, this might effect the emptying of
the stalls, which would influence the managing director more promptly
than the filling of the house with protesting pittites. This, of course,
might be dealt with as criminal conspiracy, and Mr. Yeats would
then be in his element, debating on the freedom of the Theatre as
against the freedom of the Press, and as even of more importance than
the freedom of Ireland.

ALICE L. MILLIGAN.[39]

When asked in an interview about Boyle's defection, W. B. Yeats

. . . said that Mr. Boyle evidently did not know the facts about the
new play; and, besides, he added, Mr. Boyle's own plays were treated
in the same way by the Abbey Theatre audiences when they were
first produced. He dwelt especially on 'The Building Fund', in connection with which, he said, the theatre lost many of its original
friends.

Do you think, our representative asked, that Mr. Boyle has finally
seceded from the Abbey Theatre?

No, said Mr. Yeats; certainly not. I think he has acted precipitately,
and on mere rumour; and I hope he will reconsider his position.

But how could he, if he has a fundamental objection to 'The Playboy
of the Western World'.?

Well, said Mr. Yeats, he is the last man who should take up such
an attitude; for his own admirable plays have by no means been approved of by the class of critics who are so antagonistic to Mr. Synge's.

What evidence, though, Mr. Yeats, have you of that?

Well, in the first place, I know, for instance, that we lost a great
many friends in connection with 'The Building Fund', which was
called a libel on Irish character; and, strange to say, he added, to-day
a man gave me a copy of the Christmas number of a certain Dublin
weekly which had been about the bitterest opponent of 'The Playboy',
containing an article on our plays, which says that 'The Building
Fund', 'The Eloquent Dempsy', 'The Shadow of the Glen', should be

hissed off the stage, and especially the two former, which are both by Mr. Boyle.

Well, do you think, then, that when this particular disturbance has passed over Mr. Boyle may reconsider his attitude?

I hope so, indeed, for I think he has acted

WITHOUT PROPERLY WEIGHING ALL THE FACTS

of the situation. In this connection, too, I think I may refer to the well-balanced letter in this morning's Freeman by Mr. Stephen Gwynn.

Well, I said, but what about the remarks of Mr. Wall?

Mr. Wall, said Mr. Yeats, thinks that we are behaving in a high-handed way in face of popular opposition, or rather of the opposition of portion of our audience. A very large number of the great plays of the world have been produced in the face of intense popular opposition. Ibsen's 'League of Youth', which is now the most popular of all Norwegian plays, had to face an intense opposition from the patriotic party in Norway. It is taken as a satire on the popular side, and now it is most popular with that very party—indeed with all Norway. Every student of drama has read how Moliere was treated when he wrote 'Tartuffe'. He was denounced with extraordinary violence, and was all but denied Christian burial. Fine drama, by its very nature, rouses the most fiery passions. I was told when in Paris, seven years ago, by several young Frenchmen of letters that the earlier performances of the Theatre L'euvre [sic] were followed by duels. I have myself seen the two parties shaking their fists at one another. We ourselves are passionate, and will always take things as the French take them, not as the English.[40]

On Monday, February 5, the Abbey Theatre was the scene of an open discussion of 'The Freedom of the Theatre'. Unfortunately, it did not prove a fruitful meeting:

PARRICIDE AND PUBLIC.

DISCUSSION AT THE ABBEY THEATRE.

Last night the promised discussion at the Abbey Theatre took place on the Freedom of the Theatre and 'The Playboy of the Western

World'. The proceedings were noisy, farcical, and at one period disgusting. The Theatre was crowded. Precisely to time the curtain was raised amid cheers and hisses, and Mr. W. B. Yeats, accompanied by Mr. P. D. Kenny ('Pat') appeared on the stage. 'Pat' took the chair.

Mr. W. B. Yeats, who met with a very mixed reception, said he saw it again and again said that they tried to prevent the audience from the reasonable expression of dislike. He certainly would never like to set plays before a theatrical audience that was not free to approve or disapprove ('Oh,' groans, and cries of 'What about the Police?') even very loudly, for there was no dramatist that did not desire a live audience (laughter, cheers and hisses). They had to face something quite different from reasonable expression of dissent ('Oh'). On Tuesday and on Monday nights it was not possible to hear six consecutive lines of the play. ('Quite right', and cheers), and this deafening outcry was not raised by the whole theatre, but almost entirely by a section of the pit ('Oh'), who acted together ('No. no')—and even sat together ('No'). It was an attempt to prevent the play from being heard and judged (cheers and cries of 'Quite right!').

Mr. O'Donoghue said in that day's Freeman that the forty dissentients were doing their duty (cheers), because there is no Government Censor in Ireland. The public, he said, was the Censor (cheers) where there is no other. But were these forty alone the public (groans) and the Censor? (groans). What right had they to prevent the far greater number who wished to hear from hearing and judging? (hisses and cheers). They called to their aid (cries of 'The police', and hisses) the means which every community possessed to limit the activities of small minorities who set their interests against those of the community —the police (great groaning). When the 'Countess Kathleen' was denounced with an equal violence they called in the police—that was in 1899, when he was still President of the Wolfe Tone Commemoration of Great Britain (cheers and groans). The struggle of last week had been a long necessity (cheers). Various paragraphs in newspapers, describing Irish attacks on theatres, had made many, mostly young men, come to think that the silencing of a stage at their own pleasure might win them a little fame (hisses), and, perhaps, serve their country. The last he heard of was in Liverpool (cheers), and there a stage was rushed, and a priest who set a play upon it came before that audience and apologised (cheers, and cries of 'You should have done the same'). They had not such pliant bones, and did not learn in the house that bred them a so suppliant knee ('Oh,' groans and hisses). It needed eloquence to persuade and knowledge to expound ('Oh!') but the coarser means came to every man's hand as ready as a stone or a stick (A Voice—'Or a spade', and laughter). It was not approval of Mr. Synge's play that sent the Abbey Theatre receipts up nearly £100. The generation of young men and girls who were now leaving schools and colleges were weary of the tyranny of clubs and Leagues (uproar).

The Chairman appealed to them to give a fair hearing as they expected a fair hearing for their spokesmen.

Mr. Yeats concluded by saying that manhood was all (laughter, cheers, groans, and noise).

Mr. W. J. Lawrence, who was loudly cheered, said he spoke as an Irishman and an Irish play boy (laughter and applause). He was not a member of any League or Society in Ireland. In some of his recent writings Mr. Yeats had said that praise, except it came from an equal, was an insult. He was not going to praise Mr. Yeats that night—'I come to bury Caesar, not to praise him' (laughter and cheers). He was present four nights last week, and he was present on the first occasion. Mr. Yeats was not. He was therefore in a position to speak in regard to the reception it got on the first night. He had twenty-five years' experience as a playgoer, and he had never seen a more thoroughly intellectual, representative audience. There was no predisposition to damn the play. It got a fair and honest hearing (A Voice—'It didn't on Monday', and another voice, 'Throw him out'). At the end the protest was made on the indecent verbiage, blasphemy, and Billingsgate that was indulged in (cheers, and a Voice—'Nonsense'). There was not one single call for author. That was the registration of the condemnation of the play (hear, hear). He said that viewing the reception the play got on Saturday night and the verdict of the Press that the National Theatre Society would have been well advised if they had at once, in deference to public opinion, taken the play off the boards (loud cheers). Mr. Yeats had won a Pyrrhic victory. This was not the first time in their history that a wrongly administered English law had violated Irish freedom (cheers). Mr. Yeats had struck one of the strongest blows in modern times against the freedom of the theatre (cheers). There was a movement in other countries for the abolition of censorship. If the censorship was abolished the English manager had only to adopt the method of Mr. Yeats to obtrude any indecent, vulgar play on the public. Mr. Yeat's action was an argument in favour of the creation of a censorship in Ireland (applause and dissent).

The Chairman thought they should keep within relevant limits.

Mr. Sheehy Skeffington said he was both for and against (laughter). The play was bad (hear, hear), the organised disturbance was worse (hear, hear), the methods employed to quell that disturbance were worst of all (cheers and dissent). Mr. Yeats's view would entitle him to put anything he liked on the stage and force it on his audience. As to the methods referred to when a play was rushed off the boards, such methods were, under certain circumstances, not only necessary, but the only possible methods (cheers). Mr. Yeats would have enlisted the support of the public if he had acted as he had said he would—if he had endeavoured to wear out the patience of his opponents (hear, hear). It would have been better to have enlisted the support of the public than the support of the garrison (hear, hear).

Mr. Cruise O'Brien said they protested against what they considered coercion (hear, hear). If Mr. Yeats objected to bullying so did he (cheers), and so did the audience (cheers).

Mr. T. Cuffe, rising in the pit, said there were a number of G men in the background.

Mr. Yeats, who was hissed, rose and said so far as he knew, there were no police whatever in the house (cries of 'Put them out').

Mr. O'Hoey said he was quite sure Mr. Yeats was not responsible for the presence of the G men there that night any more than for the excitement and disturbance they caused trying to create a riot amongst a handful of people outside, when they had a force sufficient to wipe them out (hisses and cheers). He thought if this play had been produced on the other side it would have been either openly or tacitly put down on the bills as a sketch of Irish peasant life (cheers). He was glad that most of those who sympathised with his view had seen fit to absent themselves that night, as a protest against the introduction of the police (cheers). There was no organised disturbance on Monday night. They objected to the attribution to the Irish people of characteristics which had not been, were not, and never would be theirs (cheers). He hoped all right-minded Irish people would teach Mr. Yeats and the management the lesson they richly deserved without further letter-writing or speeching (cheers).

Mr. R. Sheehy said their audiences when the satire was well directed and just, reproved their faults and approved the satire. Mr. Yeats claimed freedom without limits. What was to be said if, instead of slandering an individual, he slandered a nation (cheers). Mr. Yeats's position was that so long as a man paid his money and had not heard this slander, the slander must be continued until he heard it. The play was rightly condemned as a slander on Irishmen and Irish women. An audience of self-respecting Irishmen had a perfect right to proceed to any extremity (cheers).

Mr. C. P. Gavan said that he had been accused of giving information to the police last week (groans, hisses, and boos). He was referring to the moral objectors (hisses). We have a worse murderer—(the speaker's conclusion could not be heard in the storm of groans and hissing).

Mr. Beasley said he found it very hard to understand Mr. Yeats's view that night; but he found it easy last week when he (Mr. Yeats) charged him in the Police Courts (groans and cries of 'Police'). They had as chairman a gentleman who had already expressed his views in the congenial atmosphere of the 'Irish Times' (A voice—'He ought to be very impartial', and laughter.) Mr. Yeats said he came as an artist (laughter). Well, he (Mr. Beasley) hoped Irishmen would never forget his pose in the Police Court (cheers). Nature breaks out through the eyes of the cat (cheers and laughter). They had called in the claque of the garrison and police, and had rendered that place a place to which no Irishman could give the slightest support (cheers).

Mr. Molloy (Cork) said the play was not true (cheers). They protested against the squalid language poured on the stage during the last week (cheers).

Mr. J. B. Yeats said he had not read the play; he had seen it twice, but had not heard it. He knew Mr. Synge. He knew he had an affection for these people (loud laughter and cat-calls) he had described in 'Riders to the Sea'. His affection for them ('Oh,' and laughter) was based on a real knowledge ('No, no', and groans). He lived amongst them, and was their friend (disorder), and intimate with their households (cries and groans). He knew this was the Island of Saints—plaster saints (disorder and groaning). He (Mr. Yeats) was no great believer in saints, but he engaged to think that this was a land of sinners (cries of 'police, police', and laughter). The speaker went on to compare Mr. Synge's peasants and Carleton's peasants, amid much interruption. Carleton's peasants he said, were a real insult and degradation (noise), and Mr. Synge's peasant was a real, vigorous, vital man, though a sinner (loud laughter and hisses). The speaker could not proceed with the noise.

85

Mr. D. Sheehan said he came to defend the play. He did so as a peasant who knew peasants, and also as a medical student (loud laughter and groans).

The Chairman—Listen to a peasant on peasants (loud laughter).

Mr. Sheehan claimed that a man who came up and lived in Dublin for four or six years had as much right to speak of peasants as a man who lived down in the country (A Voice—'Wonderful', groans and laughter). He claimed his right to speak as a medical student (laughter), Mr. Synge had drawn a type of character that ever since he studied any science he had paid strong attention to (laughter), and that was the sexual melancholic (hisses and disorder). He said that in any country town in Ireland they would get types of men like Christy Mahon. He would refer them to the lunacy reports of Ireland (disorder), and to Dr. Connolly Norman's lectures at the Richmond Lunatic Asylum (some laughter and great disturbance). He came that night to object to the pulpit Irishman just as they objected to the stage-Irishman (renewed noise). A type of life had been brought on and held up to their praise lately in Ireland utterly unproductive altogether (cries of 'Order'). Further references to this point were received with cries of 'Shame'. Mr. Sheehan continued, when some quiet was restored. He had never seen the doctrine of the survival of the fittest treated with such living force as by Mr. Synge in his play (noise). It was they who ought to defend the women of Ireland from being un-natural pathological—(the rest of the sentence was lost in the noise). Mr. Sheehan had drawn attention to a particular form of marriage law which, though not confined to Ireland, was very common in Ireland (disorder). It was with a fine woman like Pegeen Mike (hisses) and a tubercule Koch's disease man like Shaun Keogh (some laughter, groans, hisses, and noise)—and the point of view was not the murder at all (hisses), but when the artist appears in Ireland who was not afraid of life (laughter) and his nature (boos), the women of Ireland would receive him (cries of 'Shame' and great disorder). (At this stage in the speech many ladies, whose countenances plainly indicated intense feelings of astonishment and pain, rose and left the place. Many men also retired).

Mr. Sheehan continued, but his sentences could not be followed owing to the din.

A young fellow from the stalls, under the influence of drink, here ascended the stage and tried to speak, but was removed.

Dr. Ryan said one point they were anxious to know was whether the management put forward a play as representative of the life of the West of Ireland or only a burlesque (laughter). Mr. Yeats, in the Police Court, said it was an exaggeration (a Voice—'Apropos').

A young fellow, who gave a name in Irish, said suppression was not criticism (hisses). Was the author of the play incapable of appreciating the good qualities of his country men and women? (cries of 'Yes', and cheers). The answer would be found in 'The Riders to the Sea' (hisses and noise'. If the thing was a slander the scoundrel (cheers) should be kicked out of Ireland (cheers). But they could not accept that verdict ('Yes, Yes') against a man who wrote 'The Riders to the Sea' ('Oh', and hisses). He had laid bare the strength and weakness of the Irish character (noise). There was undoubtedly a want of moral courage in our people ('Oh', and groans). They undoubtedly said one thing and think another sometimes (laughter and 'Oh').

Mr. P. Carroll said Mr. Synge's play was the result of brutal ignorance, born almost of idiocy (great noise and cheers).

Mr. W. B. Yeats asked, as to the introduction of the police, did they realise the effect upon actors of that kind of thing, of the disgraceful behaviour of Monday and Tuesday evening last ('Oh') the wear and tear of nerve, and the physical exhaustion. His business was to secure a hearing for author and actors, and to do that as quietly as possible. He had been asked why he charged Mr. Beasley. Having called in the police he thought it right and manly to go the full length (hisses). He deliberately walked down and charged a man; he did not want to charge a rowdy like some of those who were then making a noise (groans and boos). He chose a man he could respect ('Oh, oh,' and hisses). Knowing that the dispute that lay between them was one of principle (A Voice—'That won't wash'). There was one thing no one there would say he flinched from his fight (cheers). He was not a public entertainer (laughter), he was an artist (renewed laughter), setting before them what he believed to be fine works (hisses and laughter), to see and insist that they shall receive a quiet and respectful attention (laughter, hisses, and cheers).

After some disorder he arose again.

Mr. Yeats said—The author of 'Kathleen Ni Houlihan' appeals to you (cheers). They were offered support from the 'garrison' if they took 'Kathleen Ni Houlihan' from the list of their plays, and they refused (cheers), and now the author of that play, holding what he believed to be right, refused to give up the work of one whom he believed to be a man of genius (cries and laughter), because the mob cried at him

87

(cheers and noise). The groups of men and women formed a spirited section, extravagant he admitted ('Oh!'). There were two peasants in that play—one dutiful man, just such a man as Irish novelists had represented, that was the young man who would be afraid to be jealous of a man who had killed his father (groans). The other was not, he admitted, an admirable ideal, but where they had a group of girls appealed to to choose between the man who was so docile to Father Reilly and the man who killed his father, he did not think there was one woman in that room who would have hesitated (cheers and hisses). He could tell them where Mr. Synge got the central idea of the play; he would leave them to explain the facts themselves. Some ten years ago, before Mr. Synge went to the Middle Island of Arran to live there, he (Mr. Yeats) went there out of a fishing boat with Mr. Edward Martyn, Mr. Arthur Symons, and Lord Killanin. Mr. Arthur Symons had just put on record the incident. They came out of the fishing boat—a somewhat unusual thing. A crowd of people gathered around, and looking upon them as, he imagined, people flying from justice (A Voice, 'No wonder', and laughter), they brought them up to a very old man, one they said who was the oldest man on the island, and they all gathered round him in reverent admiration while he made this speech. He said if any gentleman had done a crime, we will hide him. There was a gentleman that killed his father, and I had him in my house six months till he went away to Amerikay (cries of 'Oh', laughter and cheers).

Mr. Yeats and 'Pat' then retired, and the meeting broke up with cheers and hisses and the singing of 'A Nation Once Again'.[41]

In a letter to Synge, Lady Gregory describes the meeting with different sympathies:

DEAR MR. SYNGE,—The meeting last night was dreadful, and I congratulate you on not having been at it. The theatre was crammed, all the seats had been taken at Cramers. (We made £16.) Before it began there was whistling etc. 'Pat' made a good chairman; didn't lose his temper and made himself heard but no chairman could have done much. Yeats first speech was fairly well listened to, though there were boos and cries of 'What about the police?' etc., and we had taken the precaution of writing it out before and giving the reporters a copy. No one came to support us, Russell (AE) was in the gallery we heard afterwards but did not come forward or speak. Colum 'had a rehearsal' and didn't speak or come. T. W. Russell didn't turn up. We had hardly anyone to speak on our side at all, but it didn't much matter for the disturbances were so great they wouldn't even let their own speakers be well heard. Lawrence was first to attack us, a very poor speech, his point that we should have taken the play off because the audience and papers didn't like it. . . . then a long rigmarole about a strike of the public against a rise of prices at Covent Garden, and medal which was struck to commemorate their victory. But he bored the audience. You will see the drift of the other speakers. Little Beasley was the only one with a policy for he announced his intention of never entering the place again, and called on others to do so, but the cheering grew very feeble at that point. A Dr. Ryan supported us fairly well. Though it was hard to get speakers to come forward, at the thick of the riot Mrs. Duncan sent up her name to the platform offering to give an address! But Pat sent back word he would not like to see her insulted! A young man forced his way up and argued with Dossy till a whisky bottle fell from his pocket and broke on the stage, at which Dossy flung him down the steps, and there was great cheering and laughing, and Dossy flushed with honest pride. Old Yeats made a very good speech and got at first a very good reception though when he went up there were cries of 'kill your Father', 'Get the loy', etc. and at the end when he praised Synge he was booed. The last speakers could hardly be heard at all. There was a tipsy man in the pit crying 'I'm from Belfast! Ulster aboo!' Many of our opponents called for order and fair play and I think must have been disgusted with their allies. The scene certainly justified us in having in the police. The interruptions were very stupid and monotonous. Yeats when he rose for the last speech was booed but got a hearing at last and got out all he wanted to say. He spoke very well, but his voice rather cracked once or twice from screaming and from his sore throat. I was sorry while there that we had ever let such a set inside the theatre, but I am glad today, and I think it was spirited and showed we were not repenting or apologizing. Pat came in here afterwards, very indignant with the rowdies. It is a mercy today to think the whole thing is over.[42]

The play's run had ended, and the protest demonstrations ceased, but discontent with the Abbey was evident in the press. Sinn Fein, *on the following Saturday, answers some of Yeats' statements at the open discussion:*

. . . He is reported in the daily Press as having on Monday night

89

stated that he met in the Aran Islands a person who had sheltered a man who killed his father, and that this was the basis of the play. We shall supplement Mr. Yeats's statement. The man who killed his father did exist; his name was O'Malley and he received pity and succour in his distress from the people of Inismaan. But—this Mr. Yeats did not mention—the man did not *murder* his father—he killed him by accident—the people did not glorify him for being the cause of his father's death; they pitied him in his sorrow. Out of a tragic accident, a playwright makes unnatural murder, out of human sympathy he makes inhumanity, calls it life and art, and when the people deny it to be either one or the other, he calls in the police.

Mr. Yeats has struck a disastrous blow at the Freedom of the Theatre in Ireland. It was, perhaps, the last freedom left to us. Hitherto, as in Paris or Berlin to-day, or Athens two thousand years ago, the audience in Ireland was free to express its opinion on the play. Mr. Yeats has caused that freedom to be taken away. It is the Freedom of the Theatre for the playwright to produce what he pleases and for the audience to accept or reject as it pleases. Mr. Yeats has denied the audience in Ireland the right Victor Hugo admitted when he produced 'Hernani' in Paris—the right the Greek audience always claimd and always exercised. He has wounded both art and his country. As to his country, Mr. Yeats claimed on Monday night that he had served it, and the claim is just. He served it unselfishly in the past. He has ceased to serve it now—to our regret. It is not the nation that has changed towards Mr. Yeats—it is Mr. Yeats who has changed towards the nation.

A NATIONAL THEATRE

There is a tendency in the Irish character to be distracted by minor and subordinate and often insignificant points from larger and more serious issues—and this tendency is likely to prove harmful to the national movement. The Abbey Theatre—which is a concern built and kept up by the money of an English lady, and boasts itself—'the fiddler calls the tune'—in no way more responsible to the Irish public than the police whose aid it enlists when the Irish public objects to being libelled on its stage, is in itself of small importance at all were it not that it labels itself the 'National Theatre' of Ireland. That label has now been effectively torn from it, and it may be left to the adulation of a coterie—to substitute for criticism which it seeks—it may be

90

left to the staging of squalor and the one-sided view of that which plays in the human economy the part that sewers may be held to play in the economy of the town. . . . Henry Mangan has made the excellent suggestion that such bodies as the Theatre of Ireland, the National Players' Society, the various national dramatic bodies throughout Ireland, should, with the Gaelic League, co-operate in the foundation of an Irish National Theatre. We believe the time has come for such co-operation. An Irish National Theatre will serve Ireland and serve art; but it will recognise that art evolves from the nation, not the nation from art.[43]

Also included in Sinn Fein *are two playlets satirizing the events of the previous two weeks. The first of these pieces Joseph Holloway attributes to AE:*

BRITTANIA RULE-THE-WAVE

A COMEDY

(In One Act and in Prose)

Chief Poet of Ireland. What is that sound of booing that I hear?

Chief Actor of Ireland (going to the window and looking out). I see nothing.

Chief Poet of Ireland. I must have been dreaming. We have had nothing but booing for the past week, and it has got on my nerves. I hear a hissing sound in my ears all the time. I think if we hired a policeman by the day to stand here, it would give a sense of security.

Chief Actor of Ireland. It's very expensive. I could borrow the uniform from the Castle and put one of the company in it. Would that do?

Chief Poet of Ireland. There it is again!

Chief Actor of Ireland. It's a long way off. It can't have anything to say to us. Maybe it's the Viceroy, and the boys may be giving him a welcome of that kind.

Chief Poet of Ireland. It's scandalous that he can't have a fair hearing. I would fine every man that hissed, until the Viceroy has been at least a year in office. There is no fair play in Ireland. The Viceroy is a most distinguished man, and if he is not treated with the consideration due to his rank, it will go out of Ireland that there is no true courtesy in our life. This sort of thing is killing the soul of the nation.

Chief Actor of Ireland. It's nearer now.

Chief Poet of Ireland. Send some one out to see what it is. They may be coming to attack the theatre. Ring up the police at the Exchange.

Chief Actor of Ireland. I'd better look out first. No, there's nobody! there's only a stout old lady. She couldn't make all that noise. By the holy, she's coming here. She's knocking at the door. I never saw anybody like her before. Wanting to be charwoman, maybe.

Chief Poet of Ireland. Go out and find what the hissing is about.

(Chief Actor goes out)

Chief Poet of Ireland. (murmuring to himself). 'New Commonness upon the throne'. I must re-write that, it was an appeal to the gallery. It was bad art.

(Old lady, very stout, enters. She has got a brilliant shawl round her shoulders of red and blue striped and crossed. She wears an antique bonnet of Grecian helmet shape, with horse hair on the crest, and she carries a three-pronged fork.)

Old Lady. You've a good job here.

Chief Poet of Ireland. What do you want? Where do you come from?

Old Lady. Oh, I'm very sick. I came a long way. I crossed the Channel this morning. Oh, I'm very sick.

(Chief Actor returns)

Chief Poet of Ireland. Who is she, do you think?

Chief Actor of Ireland. I don't know. She's very well got up. Maybe she's a comedy character wanting an engagement.

Chief Poet of Ireland. Do you want an engagement here?

Old Lady. Oh, I have had a hard time of it. They have hissed me through the streets. I have had a very hard time of it.

Chief Poet of Ireland. And what did they hiss you for, ma'am. Was it the play or the acting?

Old Lady. Oh, it was my beautiful play. There were miles and miles of soldiers in my play, and miles of policemen, but it never got a fair hearing.

Chief Poet of Ireland. We are just like that, we never got a fair hearing.

Chief Actor of Ireland. Would you like a job here, ma'am?

Old Lady. Yes, I would like to come here. I would like to put a lion and unicorn over the door. I would like to make it into a Royal house.

92

Chief Poet of Ireland. A Royal house! What a splendid idea. Tell me more.

Old Lady. I have many Royal houses in my own country. There were many songs made about me. Many men were knighted for love of me.

Chief Actor of Ireland. I think she's off her head.

Chief Poet of Ireland. Hush. She talks like a poet. Let us listen to her.

Old Lady. He thinks I'm off my head, but I am not; it is only the hissing that has made me sore. They will never be quiet here; they will never give me a chance here. And I am worshipped in my own country.

Chief Poet of Ireland. Who sang songs about you?

Old Lady. There was an Alfred of the Austins and a Rudyard of of the Kiplings and an Albert of the Quills. There were many hundreds of them. They will all be forgotten to-morrow, but to-morrow there will be hundreds more, and they will all sing songs for my sake. They were knighted for love of me; some of them were knighted yesterday and some will be knighted to-morrow.

Chief Poet of Ireland (eagerly). Is it in Ireland they will be knighted to-morrow?

Old Lady. Come closer to me. Let me put my shawl round you. You are like some that sang about me and were knighted long ago.

Chief Actor of Ireland. Don't listen to her. We have wasted time long enough. I don't think she would be any use to us here. They don't like her style in the theatre.

Chief Poet of Ireland. Oh, I want to listen to her. Tell me about the songs that were made about you.

Old Lady. I heard one this morning as I came over. Listen (chants)—
'They will be respectable for ever,
There shall be money in their pockets for ever,
They shall go to the Castle for ever,
The police shall protect them for ever.'

Chief Poet of Ireland. Who will the police protect?

Old Lady. Those who enter my service. Those who were pale-cheeked they will be red-cheeked. Those who were thin they will have fat paunches. Those who walked before or went in trams, will drive in carriages. Those who took off their hats will have hats taken off to them. Those who had no balance in the bank will have big balances in the bank. They will all be well paid.

Chief Poet of Ireland. What is your name, ma'am?

93

Old Lady. There are some that call me Seaghan Buidhe, and there are some that call me Brittania that Rules the Waves.

Chief Poet of Ireland. I think I have heard that name in a song.

Old Lady (going to the door). I must be going now. I must be going to the Levee. All the titled doctors in Dublin are gathering to greet me. All the heads of departments. They are the Upper classes to-day and they will be the Upper classes to-morrow. They will have no need to work. They will have no need to work (Goes out chanting): 'They will be respectable for ever,
The police will protect them for ever.'

Chief Poet of Ireland (going after her). Wait a minute. I will go with you ma'am.

Chief Actor of Ireland. Where are you going? You forget about the rehearsal here. You are forgetting you are building up a Theatre for the Nation.

Chief Poet of Ireland (in a dream). What nation are you talking about? What nationality are you going to build up. Oh, I forgot!
(Scene Shifter rushes in.)

Scene Shifter. There's a yacht in the harbour. King Edward has landed in Kingstown. The police are all going down to meet the King.

Chief Poet of Ireland (going to the door)—

Chief Actor of Ireland (detaining him). You are not going with the police. You are not going to meet the King.
(Voice is heard chanting down the stairs)—
'They will be respectable for ever,
The police will protect them for ever'.
(Chief Poet of Ireland breaks away. Chief Actor of Ireland and Scene Shifter look at each other)

Chief Actor of Ireland. Here's a holy sell. Did you see a fat old lady going down the stairs?

Scene Shifter. Faith, I did. She was the very spit of the image on the new penny. And there was a mangey old lion from the Zoo walking by her side.

(Curtain)[44]

THE FABLE OF THE FIDDLER

by 'Shanganagh' [Arthur Griffith]

There was once a Fiddler who opened a Booth in a Fair, and Over the Booth he wrote: 'The Only Genuine Irish Fiddler. The Only

94

Genuine Irish Music. Beware of Foreign Imitations. Come! Come!!
Come!!!'

The Irish Public was at the Fair. He Read the Writing, and said:
'I am glad I can at Last Hear Genuine Irish Music. I shall Beware of
Foreign Imitations. I shall Go in Here.'

And the Irish Public asked the Fiddler, 'How much.' And the
Fiddler answered—'Sixpence—same as the Foreign Imitators.'
And the Irish Public paid his Sixpence and Walked Inside.

And the Fiddler took his Fiddle and drew his Bow up and down the
Strings, and instead of emitting Music the Fiddle snarled and barked
and shrieked until the Irish Public's ears could stand it no longer,
and he said: 'But that isn't Genuine Irish Music.' And the Fiddler
replied: 'You are an Ignoramus. You don't know anything about
Ireland.'

The Irish Public was astonished, but he was a mild man, having
been Educated in the Belief that he was Full of Sin, and he said gently:

'But Surely it is not Music at all?'

'You Wretched Lout,' replied the Fiddler. 'What do you know
about Music? How dare you presume to Criticise an Artist?' And he
drew his Bow, and made the Fiddle screech till the Irish Public felt
his nerves going, and said:

'But, please, won't you play me "The Coulin," or "The Fair Hills
of Ireland." or—'

But the Fiddler with a Great Roar stood up and cried, 'You
Impudent, Ignorant, Illiterate, Interrupting Imbecile, do you not
know it is the Fiddler who Calls the Tune?'

'I really didn't know,' said the Irish Public apologetically. 'I thought
when you asked me to come here instead of going elsewhere, and when
I paid you my money that—'

'Shut up,' interrupted the Fiddler in a disgusted voice. 'What does
a Fellow like you know about Art?'

And the Fiddler rasped at his Fiddle until the Nerves of the Irish
Public gave way altogether, and he gasped—

'Well, then, won't you please stop Playing?'

This exasperated the Fiddler, and he called for the Police; and when
the Police came in, he pointed to the Irish Public, and said: 'Keep
your eye on that Scoundrel. He is an Organised Interrupter. And the
Police Smiled in Joy and drew his Baton and held it over the head of
the Irish Public, and the Fiddler rasped worse than before, so that the
Irish Public's Nerves wholly gave way and his Teeth Chattered.

95

'You heard him,' said the Fiddler to the Police, 'deliberately Interrupt.'

'But,' protested the Irish Public feebly, 'I can't help it. Your frightful rasping sets my Teeth on Edge'—and his Teeth Chattered again at the recollection, and the Police broke in his Skull with the Baton and Kicked him along the Road into a Police-Cell, and next morning brought him before the Law, who said:

'He is a Guilty-looking Scoundrel. What is the Charge?'

'I heard his Teeth Chatter when the Fiddler rasped the Fiddle,' said the Police.

'I distinctly heard him Moan,' said the Fiddler.

'Forty Shillings or a Month,' said the Law, 'and "God Save the King".'

'Hip, Hip, Hurrah for Freedom,' said the Fiddler.

Moral—This is Ireland.[45]

The Leader, too, answers one of the common defenses of the play, with a clever analogy:

. . . And yet Mr. Synge was all the while writing without any particular motive; he was merely writing to please himself and to make the people laugh. . .

A county or a country cannot, unfortunately, take a criminal libel action against a 'comedian' who intended to make its people laugh! If we worked up a sketch composed of such ingredients as a murderer, a fool, a forger, a harlot, a drunkard, an adulterer, a Freemason, an Orangeman, and such like choice specimens of West Britons, and if, to heighten the humour of the sketch, to make the matter an extravaganza, we called all the male blackguards after Mr. Yeats, Mr. Synge, and their friends, and all the female bad characters after the female relatives and friends of these gentlemen, would they object? What would they say if we told them that in objecting to the names we gave our extravaganza that was meant to make them laugh, that they were outraging literary freedom and the 'freedom of judgment,' that for our part we might have called the low women any other names, and that they were not really intended to represent Mr. Yeats' women relatives and friends, and that for the rest we did not 'care a rap. whether they felt pained or not? We suspect that under the circumstances we would hear very little from Mr. Yeats about his friends and his relatives' 'mental servitude', but would rather be the recipients of a writ for criminal libel.[46]

The most amusing by-product of the week's disturbances is the pamphlet, The Abbey Row, *which appeared within days of the riots. Joseph Holloway identified the principal author as Page Dickenson, and he adds, 'R. C. Orpen drew the frontispiece—Mrs. Grundy holding back or restraining Synge, and also the pictures of Synge and Yeats. W. Orpen drew the other two and Dickenson the last page of sketches.' Susan Mitchell wrote the poem, 'Oh, No! We Never Mention It!' The pamphlet was printed by Maunsel in a format similar to the Abbey programs and occasional publications. Although some of the jibes are really private jokes, and certain references are now obscure, the whole piece is still amusing. Serious though the implications of the Abbey riots were, in terms of the future of the national theatre, and the very nature of the artist's relations with his audience, literary Dublin could not resist seeing the humour in the quarrel.*

The shouting died down, but only for a while. In June the Abbey company brought The Playboy *on tour in England, and again there was trouble; although the English reviewers seemed surprised that anyone could have ever found the play objectionable. Even more violent protests greeted the Abbey company when it performed the play on its American tour. But the determination of the Abbey directors in continuing to present the play eventually succeeded. The quality of the play was slowly recognized, and by now none of the objections once so loudly proclaimed seem valid. Indeed, no one seemed to find it either surprising or even amusing that when the Abbey company, in 1968, had a special audience with the Pope, they presented him with a rare edition, bound in white leather of that play which once caused riots:* The Playboy of the Western World.

Notes

Introduction

1   *Freeman's Journal,* Saturday, 3 February 1906. p.7.

The 'Playboy' Riots

1   'The Abbey Theatre, "The Playboy of the Western World",' *Freeman's Journal,* Monday, 28 January 1907, p.10.
2   *Ibid.,* p.10.
3   'The Abbey Theatre: Mr. Synge's New Play,' *Daily Express* (Dublin), Monday, 28 January 1907, p.6.
4   'Public Amusements: Abbey Theatre,' *Irish Times,* Monday, 28 January 1907, p.7.
5   'Jacques,' 'A Queer Hero: in Mr. Synge's New Play. Produced at Abbey Theatre,' *Irish Independent,* Monday, 28 January 1907, p.4.
6   'H. S. D.,' 'A DRAMATIC FREAK
    FIRST NIGHT AT THE ABBEY THEATRE
    PARIS IDEAS AND PARRICIDES,' *Evening Mail,* Monday, 28 January 1907, p.2.
7   *Freeman's Journal,* Tuesday, 29 January 1907, p.7.
8   'POLICE IN
    A PLAY HOWLED DOWN
    EXTRAORDINARY SCENE IN THE ABBEY THEATRE
    PERFORMED IN DUMB SHOW
    ALL OVER A DISAPPROVED IRISH DRAMA,' *Irish Independent,* Tuesday, 29 January 1907, p.5.
9   *Evening Mail,* Tuesday, 29 January 1907, p.2.
10 'The People and the Parricide,' *Freeman's Journal,* Tuesday, 29 January 1907, p.6.
11 Manuscript 1805 in National Library, Dublin.
12 *Irish Times,* Tuesday, 29 January 1907, p.8.
13 *Evening Mail,* Tuesday, 29 January 1907, p.2.
14 *Freeman's Journal,* Wednesday, 30 January 1907, p.7.
15 *Irish Times,* Wednesday, 30 January 1907, p.6.
16 *Irish Times,* Wednesday, 30 January 1907, p.9.
17 *Irish Times,* Thursday, 31 January 1907, p.5.
18 *Freeman's Journal,* Thursday, 31 January 1907, p.7.
19 *Ibid.,* pp.7–8.
20 *Freeman's Journal,* Thursday, 31 January 1907, p.8.
21 'ABBEY THEATRE SCENES
    ANOTHER POLICE PROSECUTION
    MR. WALL AND THE INSPECTOR
    MAGISTRATE'S VIEWS
    SMALL FINE IMPOSED,' *Evening Herald,* Thursday, 31 January 1907, p.2.
22 *Freeman's Journal,* Thursday, 31 January 1907, p.8.

23 *Evening Mail,* Thursday, 31 January 1907, p.2.
24 *Irish Times,* Thursday, 31 January 1907, p.5.
25 *Evening Herald,* Thursday, 31 January 1907, p.5.
26 *Irish News and Belfast Morning News,* Thursday, 31 January 1907, p.4.
27 *Evening Mail,* Friday, 1 February 1907, p.5.
28 *Irish Independent,* 1 February 1907, p.5.
29 *Ibid.,* p.5.
30 *Ibid.,* p.5.
31 *Sinn Fein,* 2 February 1907, p.2.
32 Letter to the Editor of 'Sinn Fein', printed in *Freeman's Journal,* Friday, 1 February 1907, p.6.
33 *The Leader,* 2 February 1907, p.385.
34 *Ibid.,* pp.387–388.
35 *Freeman's Journal,* Friday, 1 February 1907, p.6.
36 *Freeman's Journal,* Saturday, 2 February 1907, p.2.
37 *Freeman's Journal,* Monday, 4 February 1907, p.4.
38 *Ibid.,* p.4.
39 *Ibid.,* p.4.
40 *Freeman's Journal,* Monday, 4 February 1907, p.4.
41 *Freeman's Journal,* Tuesday, 5 February 1907, pp.6–7.
42 Letter of Lady Gregory to J. M. Synge, undated. In National Library of Ireland, Microfilm No. 5380 (Synge Papers).
43 *Sinn Fein,* 9 February 1907, p.2. 'The Playboy of the West'.
44 *Sinn Fein,* 9 February 1907, p.3.
45 *Ibid.,* p.3.
46 'The Comedy off the Stage,' *The Leader,* 9 February 1907, pp.401–402.

Acknowledgements

The sources of the material quoted in *The Playboy Riots* are given below. Grateful acknowledgement is made to the authors and to the editors of the newspapers concerned.

Freeman's Journal: news articles dated 28, 29, 30 and 31 January 1907, and 3, 4 and 5 February 1907; letter from 'A Western Girl' 28 Jan. 1907.

Dublin Daily Express, news article dated 28 January 1907.

Irish Times, news articles on 28 and 30 January, 1907.

Irish Independent: news articles on 29 January and 1 February 1907; review by 'Jacques' on 28 Jan. 1907; and cartoons on 1 and 2 February 1907.

Dublin Evening Mail: news articles on 29 Jan. and 1 Feb. 1907; review by 'H. S. D.' on 28 Jan. 1907; and letter to editor signed 'La Lingue' on 31 January 1907.

Evening Herald: news articles dated 31 January 1907.

The Irish News and Belfast Morning News, news article dated 31 Jan. 1907.

Sinn Fein: editorials dated 2 and 9 Feb. 1907; article by 'Shananagh' (Arthur Griffith) dated 9 Feb. 1907.

The Leader: editorial on 2 Feb. 1907; article on 9 Feb. 1907; article by 'Avis', on 2 Feb. 1907.

Daily Graphic: cartoon, 1 Feb. 1907.

Padraic Colum: letter to editor, *Freeman's Journal,* 31 January 1907.

William Boyle: letters to editor, *Freeman's Journal,* 1 and 4 Feb. 1907.

Stephen Gwynn, letter to editor, *Freeman's Journal,* 2 Feb. 1907.

D. J. O'Donoghue, letter to editor, *Freeman's Journal,* 4 Feb. 1907.

Alice Milligan, letter to editor, *Freeman's Journal,* 4 Feb. 1907.

Ambrose Power, letters to editor, *Sinn Fein,* printed in *Freeman's Journal,* 1 Feb. 1907.

Joseph Holloway, Journals, Manuscript No. 1805, National Library of Ireland.

F. S. S. (Francis Sheehy Skeffington) letter to *Irish Times,* 29 Jan. 1907.

'Pat', (Patrick Kenny), review in *Irish Times,* 30 January 1907.

J. M. Synge, letter to *Irish Times,* 31 Jan. 1907.

Ellen Duncan, letter to *Irish Times,* 31 Jan. 1907.

(AE) 'Brittania Rule the Waves' in *Sinn Fein,* 9 Feb. 1907.

Lady Gregory, letter to J. M. Synge, undated, on Microfilm No. 5380, Letters to J. M. Synge, National Library of Ireland.

National Library of Ireland.